# THE FORCE IS ████████ . . .

**JACEN** loves living things. He keeps pets of all species: animals, plants, insects (some easier to care for than others . . .) and he suspects he can speak to them using the Force . . . though he doesn't quite know how.

**JAINA** takes after her father, Han. She is a mechanical whiz, always dismantling droids, machines, anything she can get her hands on. Like Han, her spirit and self-confidence sometimes get her into trouble.

**LOWBACCA,** or "Lowie," is the Wookiee nephew of Chewbacca and a native of the planet Kashyyyk. Taller than any of the others, he loves to climb to the top of Yavin 4's massive jungle trees. And on his belt, he wears . . .

**EM TEEDEE,** a translator droid built by Chewbacca to convert Wookiee speech to Basic. But because Em Teedee was programmed by See-Threepio, he tends to talk more than he has to.

**TENEL KA** is the tough, self-sufficient daughter of Teneniel Djo, one of the witches of Dathomir. Loyal, though a little humorless, she will fight beside her friends whenever they find themselves in tough situations.

This book also contains
a special sneak preview of the next *Star Wars: Young Jedi Knights* adventure:

# SHADOW ACADEMY

## ABOUT THE AUTHORS

**KEVIN J. ANDERSON** and his wife, **REBECCA MOESTA,** have been involved in many STAR WARS projects. Together, they are writing the YOUNG JEDI KNIGHTS saga, as well as creating the JUNIOR JEDI KNIGHTS series for younger readers. They are also writing a series of illustrated science books for first and second graders—THE STAR WARS COSMIC SCIENCE series—and pop-up books showcasing the Cantina scene and the Jabba's Palace scene.

Kevin J. Anderson is also the author of the STAR WARS: JEDI ACADEMY trilogy, the forthcoming novel *Darksaber*, and the comic series DARK LORDS OF THE SITH with Tom Veitch for Dark Horse Comics. His young adult fantasy novel, *Born of Elven Blood*, written with John Betancourt, was recently published by Atheneum. He has edited several STAR WARS anthologies, including *Tales From the Mos Eisley Cantina*, in which Rebecca Moesta has a story.

# STAR WARS
## YOUNG JEDI KNIGHTS

HEIRS OF THE FORCE

## KEVIN J. ANDERSON
## and REBECCA MOESTA

BOULEVARD BOOKS, NEW YORK

STAR WARS: YOUNG JEDI KNIGHTS
HEIRS OF THE FORCE

A Berkley Jam Book / published by arrangement with
Lucasfilm Ltd.

PRINTING HISTORY
Berkley Jam edition / June 1995

ISBN: 0-425-16949-9

BERKLEY JAM BOOKS®
Berkley Jam Books are published by The Berkley Publishing Group,
a division of Penguin Putnam Inc.,
375 Hudson Street, New York, New York 10014.
BERKLEY JAM and its logo
are trademarks belonging to Penguin Putnam Inc.

PRINTED IN THE UNITED STATES OF AMERICA

20   19   18   17   16   15   14   13

To our parents
—Andrew & Dorothy Anderson
and Louis & Louise Moesta—
who taught us to love books

# acknowledgments

We would like to thank Vonda N. McIntyre for helping to create the kids, Dave Wolverton for his suggestions with Tenel Ka and Dathomir, Lucy Wilson and Sue Rostoni at Lucasfilm for all their ideas and for giving us the opportunity to do this new series, Ginjer Buchanan and Lou Aronica at Berkley for being so enthusiastic about the project, and Brent Lynch, Gregory McNamee, Skip Shayotovich, and the entire STAR WARS FidoNet Echo computer bulletin board for helping out with the jokes. And special thanks to Lil Mitchell for helping with so much of the typing and to Jonathan MacGregor Cowan for Qorl's name.

# 1

JACEN SOLO HAD stayed at Luke Skywalker's Jedi academy for about a month before he managed to set up his room the way he wanted it.

Within an ancient temple on the jungle moon of Yavin 4, the student quarters were dank and dim, cold every night. But Jacen and his twin sister Jaina had spent days scrubbing the moss-covered stone blocks of their adjoining rooms, adding glowpanels and portable corner-warmers.

The son of Han Solo and Princess Leia stood now in the orangish morning light that spilled through the slit windows in the thick temple walls. Outside in the jungle, large birds shrieked as they fought for their insect breakfasts.

As he did every morning before going to Uncle Luke's lessons, Jacen fed and took stock of all the bizarre and exotic creatures he had collected out in the unexplored jungles on Yavin 4. He liked to gather new pets.

The far wall was stacked with bins and cages, transparent display cages and bubbling aquariums. Many of the containers were ingenious contraptions invented by his mechanically inclined sister. He appreciated Jaina's inventions, though he couldn't understand why she was more interested in the cages themselves than the creatures they contained.

One cage rattled with two clamoring stintarils, tree-dwelling rodents with protruding eyes and long jaws filled with sharp teeth. Stintarils would swarm across the arboreal highways, never slowing down, eating anything that sat still long enough for them to take a bite. Jacen had had a fun time catching these two.

In a damp, transparent enclosure tiny swimming crabs used sticky mud to build complex nests with small towers and curving battlements. In a rounded water bowl pinkish mucous salamanders swam formlessly, diluted and without shape, until they crawled out onto a perching shelf; then they hardened their outer membranes to a soft jellylike form with pseudopods and a mouth, allowing them to hunt among the insects in the weeds.

In another cage strung with thick, tough wires, iridescent blue piranha-beetles crawled around with clacking jaws, constantly trying to chew their way free. Out in the jungle a wild swarm of piranha-beetles could descend with a thin deadly whine. When they set upon their prey, the beetles could turn a large animal to gnawed bones in minutes. Jacen was proud to have the only specimens in captivity in his menagerie.

Often Jacen's most difficult job was not keeping the exotic pets caged but figuring out what they ate. Sometimes they fed on fruit or flowers. Sometimes they devoured fresh meat chunks. Sometimes the larger ones even broke free of their confinement and ate the *other* specimens—much to Jacen's dismay.

Unlike Jacen and Jaina's strict tutors at home on the city-covered planet Coruscant, Luke Skywalker did not depend on a rigorous course of studies. To be a Jedi, Uncle Luke explained, one had to understand many pieces of the whole tapestry of the galaxy, not just a rigid pattern set by other people.

So Jacen was allowed to spend much of his free time tromping through the dense underbrush, pushing jungle weeds and flowers out of the way, collecting beautiful insects, scooping up rare and unusual fungi. He had always had a strange and deep affinity for living creatures, much as his sister had a talent for understanding machinery and gadgets. He could coax the animals with his special Force talent, getting them to come right up to him, where he could study them at his leisure.

Some of the Jedi students—especially spoiled and troublesome Raynar—were not pleased about the small zoo Jacen kept in his room. But Jacen studied the creatures, and took care of them, and learned much from the animals.

From a small cistern Jaina had installed in the wall, Jacen ladled cool water into trays inside the cages. His motion disturbed a family of purple jumping spiders so that they hopped and bounced against the netting of the cage roof.

He ran his fingers along the thin wires and whispered to them. "Calm down. It's all right." The spiders stopped their antics and settled down to drink through their long, hollow fangs.

In another cage, the whisper birds had fallen silent, possibly hungry. Jacen would have to collect some fresh nectar funnels from the vines growing in the stones of the crumbling temple across the river.

It was almost time to go to morning lessons. Jacen tapped the sides of the containers, saying good-bye to his pets. Just before turning to leave, though, he hesitated. He peered into the bottommost container, where the transparent crystal snake usually sat coiled in a bed of dry leaves.

The crystal snake was nearly invisible, and Jacen could see it only by looking at the creature in a certain light. But now, no matter which way he looked, he saw no glitter of glassy scales, no rainbowish curve of light that bent around the transparent creature. Alarmed, he leaned down and discovered that the bottom corner of the cage had been bent upward . . . just enough for a thin serpent to slither out.

"I've got a bad feeling about this," Jacen said, unconsciously echoing the words his father so often used.

The crystal snake was not particularly dangerous—at least Jacen didn't think so. He did know from firsthand experience that the bite of the snake brought a moment of piercing pain, and then the victim fell into a deep sleep. Even though after an hour or so one would wake up and feel no ill effects, this was the sort of hazard someone like Raynar might use to cause trouble and perhaps force Jacen to move his pets to an outside storage module.

And now the crystal snake was loose.

His heart started racing with fear, but he remembered to use one of his uncle Luke's Jedi relaxation techniques to keep himself calm, to help him think more clearly. Jacen knew immediately what he had to do: he would have his sister Jaina help him find the snake before anyone noticed it was gone.

He slipped out into the dim hall, his dark round eyes flicking from side to side to check for anyone who might notice him. Then he ducked into the next rounded stone doorway and stood blinking in the shadows of his sister's room.

One entire wall of Jaina's quarters was filled with neatly stacked containers of spare parts, cyberfuses, electronic circuit loops, and tiny gears taken from dismantled and obsolete droids. She had removed unused power packs and control systems from the old Rebel war room deep in the inner chambers of the temple pyramid.

The ancient temple had once been headquarters for the secret Rebel base hidden in the jungles on this isolated moon, long before the twins had been born. Their mother, Princess Leia, had helped the Rebels defend their base against the Empire's terrible Death Star; their father, Han Solo, had been just a smuggler at the time, but he had rescued Luke Skywalker at the end.

Now, though, most of the old equipment from the empty Rebel base lay unused and forgotten by the Jedi trainees. Jaina spent her free time tinkering with it, putting the components together in new ways. Her room was crammed with so much large equipment that Jacen barely had enough space to squeeze inside. He looked around, but saw no sign of the escaped crystal snake.

"Jaina?" he said. "Jaina, I need your help!" He looked around the dim room, trying to find his sister. He smelled the sharp, biting odor of scorched fuses, heard the clunk of a heavy tool against metal.

"Just a minute." Jaina's voice echoed hollowly inside the barrel-shaped hulk of corroded machinery that took up half of her quarters. He remembered when the two of them, with the help of their muscular female friend Tenel Ka, had somewhat clumsily used their Force powers to haul the heavy machine along the winding corridors so Jaina could work on it in her room far into the night.

"Hurry!" Jacen said, feeling the urgency grow. Jaina squirmed backward out of an opening in the intake pipe. Her dark brown hair was straight and simple, tied back with a string to keep it away from her narrow face. Smudges of grease made hash marks on her left cheek.

Though her shoulder-length hair was as rich and thick as her mother's, Jaina never wanted to take the time to twist and tangle it into the lovely, convoluted hairstyles for which Princess Leia had been so famous.

Jacen extended his hand to help her to her feet. "My crystal snake's loose again! We have to find it. Have you seen it?"

She took little notice of his words. "No, I've been busy in here. Almost finished, though." She pointed down at the grimy pumping machinery. "When this is all done we'll be able to install it in the river next to the temple. The flowing water can turn the wheels and charge all of our batteries." Her words picked up speed as she began to talk. Once Jaina got started, she loved to explain things.

Jacen tried to interrupt, but could find no pause in her speech. "But, my snake—"

"With phased output jacks we can divert power to the Great Temple, provide all the light we need. With special protein skimmers added on, we could extract algae from the water and process it into food. We could even power all of the academy's communication systems and—"

Jacen stopped her. "Jaina, why are you spending all your time doing this? Don't we have dozens of permanent power cells left over from the old Rebel base?"

She sighed, making him feel as if he had missed some deeply important point. "I'm not building this because it's *useful*," she said. "I'm doing it to see if I *can*. Once I know I can do it, I won't have to waste time anymore wondering whether anything I learn here is useful or not."

Jacen was still not sure he understood. But then, his sister never could grasp his fascination for living creatures. "In the meantime, Jaina, could you help me find my snake? It's loose. I don't know where to look for it."

"All right," Jaina said, brushing her dirty hands on her stained work overall. "If the snake escaped from your room, it probably moved down the corridor."

The two of them stepped out into the long hall. Side by side, they scanned the shadows and listened.

Jacen's room was the last chamber in one of the temple passages leading to a cold, cracked stone wall. But none of the cracks was wide enough for the crystal snake to hide in.

"We'll have to check from room to room," Jaina said.

Jacen nodded. "If something's wrong, we should be able to sense it. Maybe I can use the Force to track the snake, wherever it might be hiding."

They heard the other Jedi students in their quarters dressing, washing up, or maybe just catching a few extra minutes of sleep. Jacen cocked his ears and listened, half-hoping to hear someone scream out loud, because then he would know where the snake had gone.

They slipped from room to room, pausing at closed doors. Jacen touched his fingers to the wood, but he caught no tingling sensation that might indicate his escaped pet.

But when they came to Raynar's half-open door, they immediately sensed something out of the ordinary. Peering inside, the twins spotted the boy sprawled on the polished stone tiles of the floor.

Raynar wore fine garments of purple, gold, and scarlet cloth, the colors of his noble family's house. Despite Uncle Luke's gentle suggestions, Raynar rarely took off his fancy costume, never allowed himself to be seen in drab but comfortable Jedi training clothes.

Raynar's bristly blond hair shone like flecks of gold dust in the morning sunlight spilling into his room through the window slits. His flushed cheeks sagged in and blew out as he snored softly in an awkward position on the cold tile floor.

"Oh, blaster bolts!" Jacen said. "I think we've found my snake."

Jaina slid the door closed and stationed herself by the crack so the crystal snake couldn't get past her.

Jacen knelt beside Raynar's form and let his eyelids flutter closed. He stretched his fingers into the air, and his knuckles cracked. He let his mind flow, imagining what a snake's thoughts might be like. As usual he felt many things at once through the Force, but he focused down, looking for his snake.

He sensed a slim, languid line of thought, an easily satisfied mind that right now felt cozy and safe. Its only thoughts were *warm, warm . . . sleep, sleep . . .* and *quiet.* The coiled-up crystal snake dozed beneath Raynar in the folds of his purple under-robes.

"Here, Jaina," Jacen whispered. She left the door to crouch beside him. The fabric of her stained overall hissed like another snake as she dropped to her knees.

"I suppose it's directly *under* Raynar's body?"

Jacen nodded. "Yes, where it's warmest."

"That's a problem," Jaina said. "I could roll him over, and you grab the snake."

"No, that would disturb it," Jacen said. "It might bite Raynar again."

Jaina frowned. "He'd sleep through a week's worth of classes."

"Yeah," Jacen said, "but then at least Uncle Luke could finish a lecture without getting interrupted by Raynar's questions."

Jaina giggled. "You've got a point there."

Jacen sensed the coiled snake with his mind, saw it resting peacefully; but just then, as if Raynar had heard them talking about him, the boy snorted and stirred in his sleep.

The snake surged with alarm. Jacen quickly sent out a calming message, using

Jedi relaxation techniques Luke had taught him. He sent peaceful thoughts, quieting thoughts, that calmed not only the serpent but Raynar as well.

"Working together, we could use our Jedi powers to lift Raynar up," Jacen suggested. "Then I'll pull the snake out from underneath him."

"Well, what are we waiting for?" Jaina said, looking at her brother with raised eyebrows.

Closing their eyes, the twins concentrated. They touched the fringes of Raynar's colorful robes with their fingertips as they imagined how *light* he could be . . . that he was merely a feather wafting into the air . . . that he weighed nothing at all, and they could make him drift upward. . . .

Jacen held his breath, and the still-snoring Jedi student began to rise from the tiled floor. Raynar's loose garments dangled like curtains underneath him, freeing the sleepy snake.

Suddenly deprived of its warm hiding place, the crystal snake woke up in anger, instinctively wanting to lash out. Jacen sensed it uncoiling and seeking a living target, ready to strike.

"Hold Raynar!" he shouted to Jaina as he flashed forward to snatch the slithering crystal snake. His fingers wrapped around its neck, grasping it behind the compact triangular head. He sent focused calming thoughts into the small reptilian brain, quelling its anger, soothing it.

Jacen's quick movement and release of the Force startled Jaina, and she managed to hold Raynar up for only a second or two. As Jacen worked to calm the serpent, Jaina's grip on the floating boy weakened and finally broke.

Raynar tumbled to the hard stone floor in a pile of arms and legs and garishly colored cloth. The thud of impact was enough to wake him even from a snake-drugged sleep. He sat up with a grunt, blinking his blue eyes and shaking his head.

Jacen continued to calm the invisible snake hidden in his hand. He sent tingling thoughts into its mind until the serpent fizzed with pleasure. Content, it wrapped itself around Jacen's wrist, resting its flat, transparent head on his clenched fist. Even in the best of light it barely shimmered. Its scales were like a thin film of diamonds, its black eyes like two bits of charcoal.

Groggy, Raynar looked at the dark-haired twins standing next to him. He scratched his head in confusion. "Jacen? Jaina? Well, well, well, what are you—hey!" He sat up straighter and shook his left arm as if it had gone numb. Then he glared at Jacen.

"I thought I saw one of your . . . your *creatures* in here, just for a minute. And that's the last thing I remember. Is one of your pets loose?"

Embarrassed, Jacen slid his snake-covered hand behind his back. "No," he said, "I can honestly say that all of my pets are completely accounted for."

Jaina bent down to help the other Jedi boy to his feet. "You must have just fallen asleep, Raynar. You really should have gone to your sleeping pallet if you were so tired." She brushed his clothes off. "Now look, you've got dust all over your pretty robes."

Raynar looked in alarm at the smudges of dust and dirt on his gaudy garments. "Now I'll have to put on a whole new outfit. I can't be seen in public like this!" He brushed his fingers over the cloth in dismay.

"We'll let you get changed then," Jacen said, backing toward the door. "See you at the lecture."

Jacen and Jaina ducked out of Raynar's room. Feeling suddenly bold enough to joke, Jacen waved good-bye with the hand that still carried the invisible crystal snake.

Together, the twins raced back to their quarters so they could put on their own robes in time to hear Luke teach them how to become Jedi Knights.

# 2

JAINA DUCKED BACK into her quarters to change into fresh clothes as Jacen ran to stash the crystal snake in its cage. She splashed cold water on her face from the new cistern in her bedroom wall.

Her face still damp and tingling, she stepped out into the corridor. "Hurry, or we'll be late," she said as Jacen ran to join her.

Together, the twins dashed to the turbolift, which took them to the upper levels of the pyramid-shaped temple. They entered the echoing space of the grand audience chamber. The air was a bustling hum of other Jedi candidates assembling in the huge room where Luke Skywalker spoke every day.

Shafts of morning light glinted off the polished stone surfaces. The light carried an orange cast reflected from the orange gas giant hanging in the sky—the planet Yavin, around which the small jungle moon orbited.

Dozens of other Jedi trainees of varying

ages and species found their places in the rows of stone seats spread out across the long, sloped floor. To Jaina, it looked as if someone had splashed a giant stone down on the stage, sending parallel waves of benches rippling toward the back of the chamber.

A mixture of languages and sounds came to Jaina's ears, along with the rich open-air smell that came from the uncharted jungles outside. She sniffed, but could not identify the different perfumes from flowers in bloom—though Jacen probably knew them all by heart. Right now, she smelled the musty body odors of alien Jedi candidates— matted fur, sunbaked scales, sweet-sour pheromones.

Jacen followed her to a set of empty seats, past two stout, pink-furred beasts that spoke to each other in growls. As she sat on the slick, cool seat, Jaina looked up at the squared-off temple ceilings, at the many different shapes and colors mounted in mosaics of alien patterns.

"Every time we come in here," she said, "I think of those old videoclips of the ceremony where Mother handed out medals to Uncle Luke and Dad. She looked so pretty." She put a hand up to her straight, unstyled hair.

"Yeah, and Dad looked like such a . . . such a pirate," Jacen said.

"Well, he *was* a smuggler in those days," Jaina answered.

She thought of the Rebel soldiers who had survived the attack on the first Death Star, those who had fought against the Empire in the great space battle to destroy the terrible superweapon. Now, more than twenty years later, Luke Skywalker had turned the abandoned base into a training center for Jedi hopefuls, rebuilding the Order of Jedi Knights.

Luke himself had begun training other Jedi back when the twins were barely two years old. Now he often left on his own missions and spent only part of his time at the academy, but it remained open under the direction of other Jedi Knights Luke had trained.

Some of the trainees had virtually no Force potential, content to be mere historians of Jedi lore. Others had great talent, but had not yet begun their full training. It was Luke's philosophy, though, that all potential Jedi could learn from each other. The strong could learn from the weak, the old could learn from the young—and vice versa.

Jacen and Jaina had come to Yavin 4, sent by their mother Leia to be trained for part of the year. Their younger brother Anakin had remained at home back on the capital world of Coruscant, but he would be coming to join them soon.

Off and on during their childhood, Luke

Skywalker had helped the children of Han Solo and Princess Leia to learn their powerful talent. Here on Yavin 4 they had nothing to do but study and practice and train and learn—and so far it had been much more interesting than the curriculum the stuffy educational droids had developed for them back on Coruscant.

"Where's Tenel Ka?" Jaina scanned the crowd, but saw no sign of their friend from the planet Dathomir.

"She should be here," Jacen said. "This morning I saw her go out to do her exercises in the jungle."

Tenel Ka was a devoted Jedi who worked hard to attain her dreams. She had little interest in the bookish studies, the histories and the meditations; but she was an excellent athlete who preferred action to thinking. That was a valuable skill for a Jedi, Luke Skywalker had told her—provided Tenel Ka knew when it was appropriate.

Their friend was impatient, hard-driven, and practically humorless. The twins had taken it as a challenge to see if they could make her laugh.

"She'd better hurry," Jacen said as the room began to quiet. "Uncle Luke is going to start soon."

Catching a movement out of the corner of her eye, Jaina looked up at one of the skylights high on a wall of the tall chamber. The lean, supple silhouette of a young girl edged onto the narrow stone windowsill. "Ah, there she is!"

"She must have climbed the temple from the back," Jacen said. "She was always talking about doing that, but I never thought she'd try."

"Plenty of vines over there," Jaina answered logically, as if scaling the enormous ancient monument was something Jedi students did every day.

As they watched, Tenel Ka used a thin leather thong to tie her long rusty-gold hair behind her shoulders to keep it out of her way. Then the muscular girl flexed her arms. She attached a silvery grappling hook to the edge of the stone sill and reeled out a thin fibercord from her utility belt.

Tenel Ka lowered herself like a spider on a web, walking precariously down the long smooth surface of the inner wall.

The other Jedi trainees watched her, some applauding, others just recognizing the girl's skill. She could have used her Jedi powers to speed the descent, but Tenel Ka relied on her body whenever possible and used the Force only as a last resort. She thought it showed weakness to depend too heavily on her special powers.

Tenel Ka made an easy landing on the

stone floor, her glistening, scaly boots clicking as she touched down. She flexed her arms again to loosen her muscles, then grasped the thin fibercord. With a snap from the Force she popped her grappling hook up and away from the stone above and neatly caught it in her hand as it fell.

She reeled the fibercord into her belt and turned around with a serious expression on her face, then snapped the thong free from her hair and shook her head to let the reddish tresses fall loose around her shoulders.

Tenel Ka dressed like other women from Dathomir, in a brief athletic outfit made from scarlet and emerald skins of native reptiles. The flexible, lightly armored tunic and shorts left her arms and legs bare. Despite her exposed skin, Tenel Ka never seemed bothered by scratches or insect bites, though she made numerous forays into the jungle.

Jacen waved at her, grinning. She acknowledged him with a nod, made her way over to where the twins were sitting, and slid onto the cool stone bench beside Jacen.

"Greetings," Tenel Ka said gruffly.

"Good morning," Jaina said. She smiled at the Amazonian young woman, who looked back at her with large, cool gray eyes, but did not return her smile—not out of rudeness, but because it wasn't in her nature. Tenel Ka rarely smiled.

Jacen nudged her with his elbow and dropped his voice. "I've got a new one for you, Tenel Ka. I think you'll like it. What do you call the person who brings a rancor its dinner?"

She looked perplexed. "I don't understand."

"It's a joke!" Jacen said. "Come on, guess."

"Ah, a joke," Tenel Ka said, nodding. "You expect me to laugh?"

"You won't be able to stop yourself, once you hear it," Jacen said. "Come on, what do you call the person who brings a rancor its dinner?"

"I don't know," Tenel Ka said. Jaina would have bet a hundred credits that the girl wouldn't even venture a guess.

"The appetizer!" Jacen chuckled.

Jaina groaned, but Tenel Ka's face remained serious. "I will need you to explain why that's funny . . . but I see the lecture is about to start. Tell me some other time."

Jacen rolled his eyes.

Just as Luke Skywalker stepped out onto the speaking platform, a flustered Raynar emerged from the turbolift. Puffing and red-faced, he bustled down the long promenade between seats, trying to find a place where he could sit up front. Jaina noticed the boy now wore an entirely different outfit that was as bright as the one before, and of colors that clashed just as much. He sat down and gazed up at the Jedi Master, obviously wanting to impress the teacher.

Luke Skywalker stood on the raised platform and looked out at his mismatched students. His bright eyes seemed to pierce the crowd. Everyone fell silent, as if a warm blanket had fluttered down over them.

Luke still had the boyish looks that Jaina recalled from the history tapes, but now he carried calm power in his lean form, a thunderstorm bottled up in a diamond-hard gentleness. Through many trials Luke had somehow emerged bright and strong. He had survived to form the cornerstone of the new Jedi Knights that would protect the New Republic from the last vestiges of evil in the galaxy.

"May the Force be with you," Luke said in a soft voice that nevertheless carried the length of the grand audience chamber. The words in the often-repeated phrase sent a tingle across Jaina's skin. Beside her, Jacen flashed a smile. Tenel Ka sat up rigidly, as if in homage.

"As I have told you many times," Luke said, "I don't believe the training of a true Jedi comes from listening to lectures. I want to teach you how to learn action, how to *do* things, not just think about them. 'There is no try,' as Yoda, one of my own Jedi Masters, taught me."

From the front row, in a flash of bright color, Raynar raised his hand, waggling his fingers in the air to get Luke's attention. An audible groan rippled through the chamber; Jacen heaved a heavy sigh, and Jaina waited, wondering what question Raynar would come up with this time.

"Master Skywalker," Raynar said, "I don't understand what you mean by 'There is no try.' You must have tried and failed at some time. No one can always succeed in what they want to do."

Luke looked at the boy with an expression of patience and understanding. Jaina never understood how her uncle could maintain his composure through Raynar's frequent interruptions. She supposed it must be the mark of a true Jedi Master.

"I didn't say that I never fail," Luke said. "No Jedi ever becomes perfect. Sometimes, though, what we *succeed* in doing is not exactly what we *intended* to do. Focus on what you accomplished, rather than on what you merely hoped to do. Or what you failed to do. Yes, recognize what you have lost—but look in a different way to see what you have gained."

Luke folded his hands together and walked with gliding footsteps from one side of the speaking platform to the other. His bright eyes never left Raynar's upraised face, but somehow Luke seemed to look at all of the students, speaking to every one of them.

"Let me give you an example," he said. "A few years ago I had a brilliant trainee named Brakiss. He was a talented student, a voracious learner. He had a great potential for the Force. He seemed kind and helpful, fascinated by everything I had to teach. He was also a great actor."

Luke took a deep breath, facing an unpleasant memory from his past. "You see, once it became known that I had founded an academy to teach Jedi Knights, it's not surprising that the remnants of the Empire would have their own students infiltrate my academy. I managed to catch their first few attempts. They were clumsy and untalented.

"But Brakiss was different. I knew he was an Imperial spy from the moment he stepped off the shuttle and looked around at the jungles on Yavin 4. I could sense it in him, a deep shadow barely hidden by his mask of friendliness and enthusiasm. But in Brakiss I also saw a real talent for the Force. Part of him had been corrupted long ago. He had a deep flaw surrounded by a beautiful exterior.

"But rather than reject him outright, I decided to keep him here, to show him other ways. To heal him. Because if there could be good even in the heart of my father, Darth Vader, there must also be goodness in someone as fresh and new as Brakiss." Luke gazed up at the ceiling, then returned his glance to the audience.

"He stayed here for many months, and I took special interest in teaching him, guiding him, nudging him toward the light side of the Force in every way. He seemed to be turning, softening . . . but Brakiss was colder and more deceptive than even I had suspected. During one part of his training, I sent him on an illusionary quest that would seem real to him, a test that made him face himself. Brakiss had to look inward—to see his very core in a way that no one else could ever see.

"I had hoped the test would heal him, but instead Brakiss lost that battle. Perhaps he was simply not prepared to confront what he saw inside himself. It broke him somehow. He fled from this jungle moon, and I believe he went straight back to the Empire—taking with him everything that I had taught him of the Jedi Way."

Many students in the grand audience chamber gasped. Jaina sat up and looked at her twin brother in alarm. She had never heard this story before.

Raynar again had his hand up, but Luke looked at him with narrowed eyes so full of power that the arrogant student flinched and put his hand back down.

"I know what you're thinking," Luke continued. "That I tried to bring Brakiss back to the light side, and that I failed. But—just as I told you a few moments ago—I was forced to look at how I had succeeded.

"I *did* show Brakiss my compassion. I *did* let him learn the secrets of the light side, uncorrupted by what he had already been taught. And I *did* make him look at himself and realize how broken he was. Once I accomplished that much, the task was no longer mine. The final choice belonged to Brakiss himself. And it still does."

Now he raised his eyes and looked across the gathered Jedi. As Luke's gaze passed over them, Jaina felt an electric thrill, as if an invisible hand had just brushed her.

"To become Jedi," Luke said, "you must face many choices. Some may be simple but troublesome, others may be terrible ordeals. Here at my Jedi academy I can give you tools to use when facing those choices. But I cannot make the choices for you. You must succeed in your own way."

Before Luke could continue, sudden screeching alarms rang out, sounding an emergency.

Artoo-Detoo, the little droid Luke kept near his side, rushed into the grand audience chamber, emitting a loud series of unintelligible electronic whistles and beeps. Luke seemed to understand them, though, and he leaped down from the stage.

"Trouble out on the landing pad!" Luke said, sprinting for the turbolift. He continued to speak to his students as he ran, his robes flapping behind him. "Think about what I've told you and go practice your skills."

The students milled about in confusion, not knowing what to do.

Jacen, Jaina, and Tenel Ka looked at each other, the same thought in each of their minds. "Let's go see what's going on!"

# 3

JACEN SAW THAT other Jedi students, who now rushed to the winding internal staircases or crowded into the turbolifts, had the same idea.

Tenel Ka, though, leaped to her feet and grabbed Jacen's arm, yanking him off the stone bench. "We can do it faster my way. Jaina, follow!"

Tenel Ka raced back to the stone wall below the skylights, weaving between two short lizardlike students who seemed baffled by the commotion and cheeped to each other in high-pitched voices. Already Tenel Ka had unreeled the lightweight fibercord from her belt and removed the sturdy grappling hook.

"We'll go up the wall, out the skylights, and down the outside," she said, twirling the grappling hook in her hand. The muscles in her arm rippled. At precisely the right moment she released the hook.

Jacen and Jaina helped it with the Force,

guiding the hook so that it seated properly in the moss-covered sill. Its sharp durasteel points dug into a crack in the stone blocks and held there.

Tenel Ka grasped the fibercord in both hands, tugged backward, and began to climb up the rope. She dug the toes of her scaled boots against the wall, hauling herself up, somehow finding footing on the polished stone blocks.

Jacen grabbed the rope next, holding it steady as Tenel Ka ascended like a lizard up a sunbaked cliff face. As he climbed, his arms ached. He used the Force when he needed to, raising his body up, catching himself when his feet slipped. He would have preferred to show off his physical prowess, especially with Tenel Ka watching.

At last he pulled his wiry body to the top of the Great Temple, squirming out the windowsill to stand on the broad rough-hewn platform left by the ancient builders.

Jacen reached behind him to grab his sister's arm and pulled her up. The humid air of the jungle clung to the top of the pyramid, making it hot and sticky, unlike the cool mustiness of the temple interior.

Before they could catch their breath, Tenel Ka had retrieved the fibercord and was picking her way rapidly along the narrow stone walkway. Pebbles crumbled under her feet, but she didn't seem the least bit concerned about falling.

"Around to the side," she said, not even panting. "We can get down faster that way."

Tenel Ka ran with light footsteps around the perimeter until she stopped, looking down at the cleared landing field where all ships arrived and departed. She stood stock still, like a warrior confronted with an awesome opponent.

Jacen and Jaina came up behind her and stared in amazement and horror at what they saw down in front of the temple.

A battered supply ship, the *Lightning Rod*, had landed in the jungle clearing. Their normal supply courier and message runner— long-haired old Peckhum—stood transfixed beside the open jaws of his cargo bay. His eyes were wide and white. He looked as if he had screamed himself hoarse, and could now make no sound.

He stared at a huge, unnatural-looking monstrosity that loomed out of the jungle as if ready to attack, snarling at him . . . waiting for Peckhum to make the next move.

"What *is* that thing?" Jaina asked, looking to her brother as if he would know.

Jacen squinted at the behemoth. As enormous as a shuttlecraft, its huge squarish body was covered with shaggy, matted hair tangled with primordial moss. It stood on six cylindrical legs that were like the boles of ancient trees. Its massive triangular head sat like a Star Destroyer on its shoulders, but instead of eyes inset in its skull, it had a cluster of twelve thick, writhing tentacles, each one glistening with a round, unblinking eye. Curved tusks sprouted from its mouth, long and sharp and wicked enough to tear a hole through a sandcrawler.

"It's not like anything I've ever seen in my life," Jacen said.

Tenel Ka glared down at the monster with a grim expression. "Working together, we can fight it," she said. "Follow!" She dashed down the wide-cut stone steps outside the tall temple.

The monster let out a bellow of challenge so loud and so horrendous that it seemed to make the ancient stone blocks tremble. The three young Jedi Knights hurried to the ground level, careful not to slip and fall from the steep steps.

"Help me!" Peckhum cried, his voice tinny with fright.

At the jungle's edge, the hideous monster turned, as if distracted by something. Jacen felt his heart leap, thinking at first that perhaps the wild creature had seen the three of them approaching. But he saw that its attention was fixed instead on another figure walking alone, emerging from the lower levels of the temple pyramid, confidently gliding over the clipped grasses and weeds.

Luke Skywalker wore only his Jedi robe. Jacen expected to see him holding his lightsaber, but both of Luke's hands were empty.

Luke stared at the creature, and the creature stared back with a dozen eyes waving at the ends of tentacles covering its face.

The Jedi Master continued to walk forward, directly toward the monster, as if he were in some sort of trance. He took one step, then another. The beast bristled, but held its ground, bellowing loudly enough to make the trees swish. Jungle birds and creatures fled from the horrifying sound.

While the beast was momentarily distracted, old Peckhum dove to the ground, scuttling on all fours through the open cargo doors of his battered shuttle. Jacen was glad to see the supply runner safe inside the shielded metal walls.

The monster roared upon losing its prey. But Luke spoke in an oddly calm and clear voice that was not at all muffled by the distance. "No, here! Look at me," he said.

Tenel Ka reached the ground by leaping down the last four steps and landing in a crouch. Puffing and red-faced, Jacen and Jaina dashed down beside her, then all three teens stood rigid, watching Luke Skywalker face the jungle beast. They had no weapons of their own.

Suddenly, unexpectedly, old Peckhum charged back out of the open bay doors of the *Lightning Rod*. In his hands he held an old-fashioned blaster rifle. "I'll get him, Master Skywalker! Just stay there." He ducked down and aimed.

But Luke turned to him and motioned with his hand. "No," he said.

The blaster rifle went flying out of Peckhum's grip. The old supply runner stared in astonishment as Luke continued to stroll toward the monster, seemingly without a care in the world.

"This creature means no harm," Luke said, his voice quiet but firm. He never took his eyes off the beast. "It's just frightened and confused. It doesn't know where it is, or why we are here." He drew a deep breath. "There's no need for killing."

Jacen's stomach knotted with unbearable tension as Luke approached the monster. The thing's long eyestalks waved at him, and its six tree-trunk legs took ponderous steps like an Imperial walker.

The beast lowered its triangular head, shaking it from side to side so that the pointed tusks seemed to scratch holes in the air. It let out a strange, soft *blat* of puzzlement.

Jacen hissed with fear, and his sister's entire body clenched. He had used his own talents with the Force to confront many strange animals out in the jungle, but never anything as powerful as this monster, never such a boiling mass of anger and confusion.

But Luke stepped right up to the shaggy, angry thing, within touching distance. The Jedi Master looked incredibly small, yet unafraid.

Beside the battered freighter, Peckhum fell to his knees. The discarded blaster rifle was at hand, but he didn't dare pick up the weapon again. He looked from the monster to Luke, then to the three watching teens— then off into the jungle, as if terrified that another one of the creatures might appear.

Luke stood in front of the nightmarish beast and took a deep breath. He didn't move. The monster held its ground and snorted. Its eyestalks waved unblinking, pointing slitted pupils down at him.

Luke raised his hand, palm out.

The monster snuffled and waited, motionless, its wicked tusks less than a meter away from Luke Skywalker.

The jungle fell silent. The breeze died away. Jacen held his breath. Jaina gripped his hand. Tenel Ka narrowed her cool gray eyes.

The silence seemed so overwhelming that

when Luke at last broke the frozen moment, his whisper sounded as loud as a shout.

"Go," Luke told the creature. "There is nothing you need here."

The monster reared up on its hind set of piston legs, its eye tentacles thrashing in a frenzy. Then it let out another high-pitched trumpet before it spun around and crashed off into the thick undergrowth. Branches cracked, trees bent to one side as it plowed a wide path back to the mysterious jungle depths from which it had come.

Like a snapped string, Luke's shoulders slumped with exhaustion. He seemed barely able to keep himself from trembling as Jacen, Jaina, and Tenel Ka rushed toward him, calling his name. "Uncle Luke!"

Luke turned and looked at the three friends with a smile.

Old Peckhum stumbled up, clutching the antiquated blaster rifle. His eyes glittered with unshed tears. "I can't believe you did that, Master Skywalker!" he said. "I thought I was dead for sure, but you faced that monster with no weapons at all."

"I had enough weapons," Luke said with calm conviction. "I had the Force."

"I wish I could do that, Uncle Luke," Jacen said. "That was really something."

"You will be able to do anything you want,

Jacen," Luke said. "You have the potential—as long as you have the discipline."

Luke gazed off into the jungle, where they could still hear trees crashing and shrubs snapping as the monster continued to blunder its way through the forest.

"There are many mysterious things in the jungles," Luke said, then he smiled at the twins and Tenel Ka. He nodded toward Peckhum's ship, the *Lightning Rod*, which still sat open, filled with crates and boxes of supplies and equipment.

"I think our friend Mr. Peckhum is having a rough day," Luke said. "He's got a lot more to unload, and he's probably eager to get back up into orbit, where it's safe." He flashed a smile at the old supply runner, who nodded vigorously.

"Why don't you three consider it a Jedi training exercise to help him. Besides, we need to get ready because tomorrow—" He looked at Jacen and Jaina, eyes sparkling. "Your father and Chewbacca are bringing us another Jedi trainee."

"Dad's coming here?" Jaina said with a yelp.

"Hey, why didn't you tell us before?" Jacen added. His heart leaped at the thought of seeing his father again after a full month.

"I wanted it to be a surprise. He's flying in on the *Millennium Falcon*, but he had to stop at Chewbacca's planet first. They've already left Kashyyyk, and they're on their way here."

Filled with excitement, the young Jedi Knights eagerly helped unload Peckhum's supply ship. It was hard work, demanding more concentration and control of their Jedi lifting abilities than they were used to, but they finished in less than an hour. Jaina and Jacen chattered to Tenel Ka about all the adventures Han Solo had experienced. Jaina groaned about how much work it would be to clean up their quarters in time, so they could impress their father.

Finally, the battered old freighter flew off into the misty skies toward the orangish gas-giant planet of Yavin.

Jacen smiled and looked wistfully at the trampled clearing. The next ship to arrive on the landing pad would be the *Millennium Falcon*!

# 4

"THERE," SAID JAINA, mentally relaxing her hold on a large mass of tangled wires and cables. It came to rest in a more or less contained jumble atop one of the newly tidied stacks of electronic components in her room. "That should do it," she added with a satisfied nod.

"Does that mean we can go to morning meal now?" Jacen said. "You've been at this half the night."

"I want Dad to be impressed." Jaina shrugged.

Jacen laughed. "He never stacks *his* tools this neatly!"

"Guess I did get a little carried away," Jaina replied, matching his grin. "We've still got a few hours before they get here."

Jacen snorted and stood up from the floor, where he'd been sitting next to his sister while they worked. He brushed the dust off his jumpsuit and ran long fingers through his dark brown curls. "Well, how do I look?"

Jaina raised a critical eyebrow at him. "Like someone who's been up all night."

He hurried over to peer anxiously into the small mirror that Jaina had hung above her cistern. She realized that her brother was just as nervous and excited about seeing their father again as she was.

"It's actually not too bad," she assured him. "I think raking the twigs and leaves from your hair really helped. Here, put this on." She pulled a fresh jumpsuit from a chest by her bed. "You'll look more presentable."

When Jacen went into the next room to change, Jaina took his place at the mirror. She wasn't vain, but, as with her room, she preferred to keep her personal appearance neat and clean.

She ran a comb through her straight brown hair and stared at her reflection. Then, with a quick peek over her shoulder to be sure her brother wasn't looking, she pulled back a handful of strands and worked them into a braid. Jaina would never have gone to this much trouble for an ambassador or some silly dignitary—but her father was worth the effort. She hoped Jacen wouldn't notice or comment on it.

Finished, she stepped through her doorway and poked her head into Jacen's room. "All the animals fed?" she asked.

"I took care of that hours ago," he said, emerging in his clean, fresh robe. He heaved a long-suffering sigh. "At least *someone's* had their morning meal."

Jaina gnawed her lip, anxiously scanning the sky for any glimmer that might herald the arrival of the *Millennium Falcon*. She and Jacen stood at the edge of the wide clearing in front of the Jedi academy, where the hideous monster had appeared the day before. The area's short grasses had been trampled down by frequent takeoffs and landings.

Jaina smelled the rich green dampness of the early morning in the jungle that surrounded the clearing. The foliage rustled and sighed in a light breeze that also carried the trills, twitters, and chirps that reminded her of the wide profusion of animal life that inhabited the jungle moon.

Beside her, Jacen shifted impatiently from one foot to the other, a frown of concentration etched across his forehead. Jaina sighed. Why did it seem like everything took forever when you were looking forward to it, and things that you didn't want to happen arrived too soon?

As if sensing her tension, Jacen suddenly

turned to her with a mischievous look in his eye. "Hey, Jaina—you know why TIE fighters scream in space?"

She nodded. "Sure, their twin ion engines set up a shock front from the exhaust—"

"No!" Jacen waved his hand in dismissal. "Because they miss their mothership!"

As was expected of her, Jaina groaned, grateful for a chance to get her mind off waiting, even if only for a moment.

Then a comforting hum built and resonated around them, as if the sound of their mounting excitement had suddenly become audible. "Look," she said, pointing at a silver-white speck that had just appeared high above the treetops.

The glimmer disappeared for a few moments and then, with a rush of exhaled breath that she hadn't realized she'd been holding, Jaina saw the *Millennium Falcon* swoop across the sky toward the clearing.

The familiar blunt-nosed oval of their father's ship hovered tantalizingly above their heads for a moment that seemed to stretch to eternity. Then, with a burst of its repulsorlifts, it settled gently onto the ground in front of them. The *Falcon*'s cooling hull buzzed and ticked as the engines died down to a low drone. The scent of ozone tickled Jaina's nostrils.

Jaina knew the shutdown procedures for

the Corellian light freighter, but she wished that just for today there was some way to speed things up. When she thought she could wait no longer, the landing ramp of the *Falcon* lowered with a whine-thump.

And then their father bounded down the ramp, gathering the twins into his arms, ruffling their hair, and trying to hug both of them at once, as he had done when they were small children.

Han Solo stepped back to take a good look at his children. "Well!" he said at last, with one of those lopsided grins for which he was so famous. "Except for your mother, I'd say this is the finest welcoming committee I've ever had."

"Dad," Jacen said, rolling his eyes, "We are *not* a committee."

As her father laughed, Jaina took a moment to study him, and was relieved to note that he had not changed in the month that they had been gone from home. He wore soft black trousers and boots that fitted him snugly, an open-necked white shirt, and a dark vest—a comfortable, serviceable set of clothes that he sometimes jokingly referred to as his "working uniform." The battered, familiar shape of the *Millennium Falcon* was unchanged as well.

"How do we look, Dad?" Jaina asked. "Any different?"

"Well, now that you mention it . . ." he said, turning his gaze to each of them in turn. "Jacen, you've grown again—bet you even caught up with your sister. And Jaina," he said with a wicked grin, "if I didn't think you'd throw a hydrospanner at me for saying so, I'd tell you that you're even prettier than you were a month ago."

Jaina blushed and gave an unladylike snort to demonstrate what she thought of such compliments, but secretly she was pleased.

A loud, echoing roar from inside the ship saved her the embarrassment of having to come up with a response. A large form thundered down the boarding ramp. Huge heavily furred arms reached out to grab Jaina and threw her high into the air.

"Chewie!" Jaina shrieked, laughing as the giant Wookiee caught her again on the way down. "I'm not a little kid anymore!" After Chewbacca had repeated this greeting ritual with her brother, Jaina finally said what she and Jacen were thinking. "It's good to see you, Dad, but what brings you to the Jedi academy?"

"Yeah," Jacen added. "Mom didn't send you to check if we had enough clean underwear, did she?"

"Nah, nothing like that," their father assured them with a laugh. "Actually, Chewie and I needed to come out this direction to help my old friend Lando Calrissian open up a new operation."

Jaina had always had a great fondness for Lando, her father's dark and dashing friend, but she also knew him well enough to realize that her adopted "uncle" Lando was always involved in some crackpot moneymaking scheme or another. She held up a hand to stop her father.

"Wait, let me guess. He's—he's starting a new casino on his space station and he needed you to bring him a shipload of sabacc cards."

"No, no, I've got it," Jacen said. "He's opening a new Nerf ranch and he wants you to help him build a corral."

At this Chewbacca threw back his head and bleated with Wookiee laughter.

"Not even close." Han Solo shook his head. "Corusca gem mining deep in the atmosphere of the gas giant." He pointed up to the great orange ball of the planet Yavin in the sky overhead. "He asked us to come and help him set up the operation."

"Oh, blaster bolts!" said Jacen, snapping his fingers. "That was going to be my next guess."

Another faint Wookiee-sounding bellow came from inside the *Millennium Falcon*. Chewbacca turned and strode back up the ramp.

"What was that?" Jaina asked.

"Oh, I forgot to mention," Han said. "When Luke found out we had to come here anyway, he asked us to stop by Chewie's homeworld of Kashyyyk and pick up a new Jedi candidate. He's going to be your fellow student."

As Han spoke, Chewbacca thumped back down the ramp, closely followed by a smaller Wookiee, who was still taller than Jacen or Jaina. The younger Wookiee had thick swirls of ginger-colored fur, with a remarkable swirling black streak as wide as Jaina's hand that ran from just above his left eye up over his head and down to the middle of his back. He wore only a belt woven of some glossy fiber that Jaina could not identify.

"Kids, I'd like you to meet Chewie's nephew Lowbacca. Lowbacca, my kids Jacen and Jaina."

Lowbacca nodded his head and growled a Wookiee greeting. He was thin and lanky, even for a Wookiee, with gangly fur-covered arms and legs. The young Wookiee fidgeted. Chewbacca barked a question to Han and waved one massive arm in the direction of the temple.

"Sure," Han said. "Go ahead—take him to Luke for now. The kids can get to know each other later."

As the two Wookiees headed off to find Luke, Han said, "Wait here, I have something for you," and ducked back into the *Falcon*. He returned in a few moments, his arms laden with a strange assortment of packages and greenery.

"First," he said, tossing each of them a small message disk, "your mother recorded these personal holo letters for you. There's another one from your little brother Anakin. He can't wait to come here himself."

Jaina looked at the glittering message disks, anxious to play them. But she slipped them into one of the pockets of her jumpsuit.

"And now . . ." Han said, holding up a large bouquet of green fronds sprinkled with purple and white star-shaped blossoms. Grinning, he waggled the flowers.

"Oh, Dad, you remembered!"

Jacen ran forward ecstatically. "My stump lizard's favorite food." He took the leafy bundle gratefully and said, "I'll feed 'em to her right away. See you later, Dad." Then he ran off in the direction of the Great Temple.

Jaina stood alone with her father, looking expectantly at the last bulky package he held in his arms. He set it on the weedy ground of the landing clearing and stepped back so that Jaina could pull aside the rags that covered it.

"Great wrapping job, Dad," she said, smiling.

"Hey, it works." Han spread his hands.

Jaina gasped as she removed the coverings, then looked up at her father, who grinned and shrugged nonchalantly. "A hyperdrive unit!" she said.

"It's not in working condition, you understand," he said. "And it's pretty old. I got it off an old Imperial Delta-class shuttle they were dismantling on Coruscant."

Jaina remembered fondly the times she had helped her father tinker with the *Falcon*'s subsystems to keep it running in peak condition—or as close as they could get. "Oh, Dad, you couldn't have picked a better present!" She jumped up and hugged him, wrapping her arms around his dark vest. She could tell that her father was pleased—and maybe even a little embarrassed—by her enthusiasm.

Her father looked down at her and raised one eyebrow. "You know, there's a couple more components on the ship. If you wanted to help me bring 'em out here, your dad could show you how they all go together."

She ran after him into the ship.

# 5

IT WAS LATE that morning when Jacen and Jaina finally caught up with their father, Chewbacca, and his nephew Lowbacca. The twins, who had spent hours at their respective assigned duties and Jedi training exercises, arrived back at the students' quarters just as they saw the threesome emerge from a formerly empty room.

"Hi!" Jacen called, hurrying up to Lowbacca with his sister in tow. "Are you tired from your trip? If not, I could show you my room. I have some really unusual pets. I collected most of them from the jungles here and Jaina made some cages for them—you should see those cages—and Jaina could show you her room too. She's got all sorts of broken-down equipment that she uses to build things out of." In his enthusiasm, Jacen never even paused to take a breath.

The much taller Lowbacca looked down at the human boy as Jacen rattled on. "Do you like animals? Do you like to build things? Did you bring any pets or equipment with you from Kashyyyk? Do you like—"

His father chuckled into the stream of questions. "There'll be time enough for that later, kid. We spent most of the morning with Luke, and then we got Lowbacca settled in his room. You two want to take him on a tour of the academy, get him familiar with the place? By now, you probably know your way around better than Chewie or I do."

"We'd love to," Jaina answered before their father had finished his sentence.

"We're the perfect tour guides," Jacen added with a confident shrug. "Jaina and I came to the Jedi academy for the first time when we were only two years old." He smiled a cocky, lopsided grin—the one their mother always said made him look just like his father.

Lowbacca gave an interrogative growl. "He asked how many times you've given this tour," Han translated.

"Well," Jacen sputtered, his face reddening slightly, "if you mean in an *official* capacity, as opposed to, er, um . . ." His voice trailed off.

"What he means is," Jaina put in firmly, "this is our first time."

Lowbacca exchanged a glance with his uncle. Chewbacca raised a furred brown

arm, indicated the long corridor with a flour-
ish of his hand, and gave a short bark.

"Right," Han said. "Let's go."

The twins led the group down a set of
mossy, cracked stairs to the main level and
out onto the grassy clearing in front of the
Great Temple. Jacen was eager to prove himself a good tour guide and pointed to each
squarish level of the gigantic pyramid as he
spoke.

"At the very top is an observation deck that
gives one of the best views of the big planet
Yavin overhead—unless of course you climb
one of those huge old Massassi trees in the
jungle," he said with a laugh. "The top level
of the pyramid has only one enormous room—
the grand audience chamber—that can hold
thousands of people."

"That's where the Jedi trainees gather
when Uncle Luke—I mean Master Skywalker—gives his lessons," Jaina said.

Jacen went on to explain that the lower
levels had been remodeled in recent years.
The larger level directly below the grand
audience chamber housed those who lived at
the academy—trainees, academy staff, and
Master Skywalker himself—and also contained rooms for storage or meditation, as
well as chambers for guests and visiting
dignitaries.

The pyramid's huge ground level held the Communications Center, the main computers, meeting areas and offices, and common rooms in which meals were prepped and eaten. It also held the Strategy Center—the chamber that had been known as the War Room in the days when the temple had housed the Alliance's secret base. Underground, and completely invisible from where they stood, was a gigantic hangar bay that stored shuttles, speeders, fighters, and other aircraft.

On two sides of the Great Temple and along the landing area flowed broad rivers, and beyond them lay the lush and mostly unexplored jungles of the fourth moon of Yavin. "The temples were built by the Massassi, a mysterious ancient race. There are actually lots of structures scattered throughout the jungles," Jacen said. "Some of them are just ruins, really—like the Palace of the Woolamander across the river there."

He described the power-generating station next to the main temple, a series of plate-shaped wheels, twice as tall as Jacen himself, standing on edge and connected through the center by a long axle.

"So you see," Jaina said, picking up the narration where her brother had left off, "with the power station, the river, and the jungles, the Jedi academy is fairly self-sufficient. Come on, let's go inside."

The tour concluded at the twins' quarters, where Jacen and Jaina delighted in showing their father and the two Wookiees their respective treasure troves of pets and salvaged bits of machinery. Han Solo beamed with fatherly pride. Lowbacca displayed a gratifying if subdued interest in the creatures in Jacen's menagerie.

When the group moved into his sister's room, Jacen quickly slid the crystal snake he had been showing off back into its cage and hurried after them. By the time he bounded through the door, Lowbacca was already engrossed in an assortment of gadgets and wiring that he had spread out across Jaina's floor. He was far more interested in the electronics than in the wild jungle creatures.

"Do you like working on machines, Chewie—uh, I mean, Lowbacca?" Jaina asked, bending next to the gangly Wookiee.

The hairy creature expressed his fascination with such a long series of grunts, growls, and rumbles that Jacen was at a loss to understand how a simple yes-or-no question could produce such an animated answer.

As usual, their father translated. "First of all, Lowbacca would take it as a great sign of friendship if you would call him Lowie."

Jacen gave a pleased nod. "'Lowie,' huh? I like that."

"And for the rest . . ." Han continued, "well, I'm not sure I followed it all. The thing he really gets excited about is computers."

Jaina patted the young Wookiee on the shoulder. "We can do a lot of things together, then, Lowie." Chewbacca chuffed in agreement.

But Jaina's forehead furrowed with sudden concern. "Uh, Dad?" she said. "It's obvious that Lowie has studied our language and understands us as well as Chewie does. But we can't understand *him*. After all, it took you years to learn the Wookiee language. How is he going to get by here at the Jedi academy where nobody can understand him?"

Jacen nodded agreement, looking at the young Wookiee. "Who'll translate for us?"

They were interrupted at this point by a triumphant bark from Chewbacca.

"We have just the answer for you," Han said, clapping his hands and rubbing them together. "A little something that See-Threepio and Chewie cooked up."

Chewbacca turned and held out a shiny metallic device for everyone to see. The sidewise-ovoid apparatus was silvery, slightly longer than Lowie's hand and about four fingers thick, flat on the back and rounded on the front. It looked like a face, with two yellow optical sensors unevenly spaced near the top, a more or less triangular protrusion toward the center, and a perforated oblong on the lower portion that Jacen took to be a speaker.

Chewbacca fiddled with something at the back of the device, and the yellow eyes flickered to life. A thin metallic voice, careful and correct, issued from the tiny speaker. "Greetings. I am a Miniaturized Translator Droid—Em Teedee—specializing in human-Wookiee relations. I am fluent in over *six* forms of communication. My primary pro-grammed function is to translate Wookiee speech into other humanoid languages." It paused expectantly and then added, "Might I be of assistance?"

Jacen laughed. "It can't be!"

Jaina gasped. "Sounds just like Threepio!"

"Almost," their father replied, his mouth twisted in wry amusement. He scratched under his collar with one lazy finger. "A little *too much* like Threepio, for my money. But since he did most of the programming on Em Teedee, I couldn't talk him out of it." He shrugged apologetically.

"Why don't you kids try it out during the midday meal? Chewbacca and I still have some business to discuss with Luke, then we'll take off in the *Falcon* later this afternoon. We've got to see Lando at his mining station."

The common room the Jedi trainees used as a mess hall was filled with wooden tables of various heights. The seats—chairs, benches, nests, ledges, cushions, and stools—came in a broad variety of shapes and sizes to accommodate the differing customs and anatomies of human and alien students.

The plantlike members of the Jedi academy had gone outside to the bright sunwashed steps of the Great Temple, where they could soak up light from Yavin's white sun and photosynthesize for nutrients, adding small packets of minerals into their digestive orifices. Inside the mess hall, though, dozens of unusual species sat together eating exotic foods particular to their own kind.

Jacen followed a step behind, still chattering about the old Massassi temples, as Jaina found a table at one end of the large hall that had a chair appropriate for Lowbacca. So far Jacen had been unable to elicit more than a few nods and gestures from the Wookiee, who seemed deep in thought, intent on absorbing the smells, sights, and sounds around him.

Determined to start a real conversation with the new trainee, Jacen cast about in his mind for a good question. *So, Lowie, how much stuff do you need to move in?* Naw, that was a stupid question.

How about, *How old are you?* No, that would get him only a short answer. And anyway, their father had told them that earlier this morning. Lowie was nineteen, barely an adolescent by Wookiee standards. Maybe something like, *How did you know you wanted to become a Jedi?* Yes, that was good.

But before he could pose the question, the solid, muscular form of Tenel Ka swung into the seat next to him, across from Lowbacca.

"New student," she said, acknowledging Lowbacca in the brief, direct way that was so characteristic of her.

"Lowie," Jacen said, "this is our friend Tenel Ka, from the planet of Dathomir."

"And this," Jaina responded, making the introductions for her side of the table, "is Lowbacca, nephew of Chewbacca, from the Wookiee homeworld of Kashyyyk."

Tenel Ka rose formally and inclined her head, tossing her red-gold hair. "Lowbacca of Kashyyyk, I greet you," she said, and resumed her seat. Lowbacca nodded in return and uttered three short growls.

Jacen waited for a moment, looking at the little translator droid clipped to Lowie's belt, but nothing happened.

"Well?" Jaina said expectantly. "You going to translate for us, Em Teedee?"

"Goodness me, Mistress Jaina, I *am* sorry," the tiny droid replied in a flustered, mechanical voice. "Oh, how dreadful! My initial opportunity to perform my primary function for Master Lowbacca, and I've failed him. I assure you, masters and mistresses all, that from now on I will endeavor to make each translation as speedily and as eloquently as possible—"

Lowbacca interrupted the translator droid's self-reproach with a sharp growl.

"Translate?" the little droid replied. "Translate what? Oh! Oh, I see. Yes. Immediately." Em Teedee made a noise that sounded for all the world as if it was clearing its throat, and then began. "Master Lowbacca says, 'May no sun rise upon a day, nor any moon rise upon a night, in which he is not as honored to see you, and to be in your presence, as he is at this very moment.'"

Jaina rolled her eyes. Jacen shook his head in disbelief. But Tenel Ka's face remained expressionless.

From the corner of his eye, Jacen caught sight of the troublesome young student Raynar in his colorful robes, snickering at them from a nearby table. Automated servers carried generous bowls of food from the kitchen and placed them in front of each trainee.

But Jacen's attention was brought back to his own table when Lowie growled down into the optical sensors of the translator droid.

"Well, so what if I *did* embellish a bit?" the droid asked defensively, as a plate of steaming, blood-red meat was placed in front of the Wookiee. "I was only attempting to make you sound more civilized."

Lowbacca's threatening growl left no doubt as to whether he was grateful to the droid.

"Very well," Em Teedee huffed. "Perhaps a better translation of Master Lowbacca's words would have been, 'The sun has never shined so brightly for this humble Wookiee as on this day we meet.'"

Jacen accepted a hot cup of soup that his sister passed across the table to him. He shot a questioning look at Lowie, who growled again at Em Teedee.

"Well, have it your way then," the droid said haughtily, but in a more subdued voice. "But I assure you that my translations were much more refined. *Ahem*. What Master Lowbacca *actually* said was, 'I am pleased to meet you.'"

When the Wookiee finally grunted in satisfaction, Tenel Ka replied gravely, as if she had not heard any of the other translations, "It is a pleasure shared, Lowbacca."

As an automated tray trundled past toward

Raynar's nearby table, Tenel Ka reached out and snagged the last jug of fresh juice. She poured the rich ruby liquid into each of their cups and then set the jug with a gentle *thump* on the table before them. She blinked her cool gray eyes and solemnly held out her cup.

"Jacen and Jaina are already my friends. I offer you friendship, Lowbacca of Kashyyyk."

The Wookiee hesitated, unsure of what to do. Jaina pressed a cup into his hand. Jacen raised his and said, "Friendship."

"Friendship," Jaina echoed.

Nodding, Lowie lifted his glass high in the air, threw his head back, and let out a roar that rang through the hall.

The small voice of Em Teedee broke the silence that followed. "Master Lowbacca most emphatically accepts your offer of friendship and extends his own." To everyone's surprise, the Wookiee did not correct the translator.

"Accepted," Tenel Ka said, taking a drink. When everyone had followed suit, she said, "And now we are friends."

"That means you can call him Lowie now," Jaina said.

Tenel Ka considered this for a moment. "I choose to honor him by using his complete name."

At another table, three short reptilian

Cha'a sat around a trayful of warm, rocking eggs, staring fixedly at them like the predators they were. When the eggs cracked and opened, the Cha'a lunged for the bright pink furry hatchlings as they emerged fresh from the shells.

Two whistling avian creatures shared a plateful of thin, writhing threads covered with fluffy blue hair—tantalizing ropy caterpillars which they slurped one at a time through their narrow, horny beaks.

As Jacen sat at the table spooning his soup, trying to think of something amusing to say to Tenel Ka, or at least to continue the conversation with Lowie, he caught a glimpse of movement out of the corner of his eye—something slithering toward the table beside them. A glassy glitter. A serpentine flash.

Jacen's heart leaped into his throat. He suddenly wondered if he had fastened the cage of the crystal snake when his father and the Wookiees had finished their tour of his chambers.

"Hey," Raynar said, leaning over the table beside them, his flashy robes so brilliant that they made Jacen's eyes ache. "Would you mind giving our juice jug back?" Raynar used his own Jedi powers to snatch the jug from their table and carry it through the air back toward himself. "Next time please ask before you just take it." He leaned back and crossed his arms over his chest with a self-satisfied expression.

Just then, light fell on the crystal snake, and Jacen saw it with perfect clarity. It reared up on Raynar's lap and hissed at him, its flat triangular head staring the boy right in the face.

Raynar saw it and shrieked, losing his Force concentration. The jug wobbled, then fell, spilling deep red juice all over his bright robes.

Jacen leaped to his feet and jumped for the snake. He had to catch it before it wreaked more havoc. He tackled Raynar, trying to grab the serpent from the other boy's lap. Raynar, thinking he was being attacked from all sides, screamed in terror at the top of his lungs.

As he and Jacen struggled, their entire table toppled over, spilling dark brown pudding, knocking other beverage containers right and left, spraying food on Raynar's companions at the table.

Tenel Ka, not understanding the problem but always ready to defend her friends, jumped into the fray. She picked up Jacen's hot soup and hurled it toward Raynar's companions, who, seeing the attack coming from a new front, decided to retaliate.

A platter of honeyed noodles sailed across

the dining hall toward Jaina, but she ducked. The noodles instead splattered and clung to the bristly white fur of a Talz—a bearlike creature that stood up and blatted a musical note of dismay. When Jaina saw the noodles sticking to the alien's white fur, she couldn't stop herself from laughing.

The crystal snake slithered out of Jacen's grasp as Jacen crawled across Raynar's squirming lap. The young Jedi screamed as if he were being murdered, but Jacen scuttled under the dining tables after the serpent. Bumping one of the tables over while grabbing for the snake, he felt smooth, dry scales against his fingertips—but the snake slid through them, and he could not hold on.

Another table was knocked over as Lowie came to help. With a flurry of feathers, the avian creatures squawked and fought over their plateful of squirming, fuzzy blue thread-worms.

More food flew through the air, levitated by Jedi powers, and tossed from one table to another. The Jedi students were laughing, seeing it now as a release from the tension of the grueling studies and deep concentration required of them during their training.

Steamed leaves flew in the faces of the reptilian Cha'a, interrupting their predatory concentration. All three of them stood up and whirled to meet the attack, back-to-back, standing in a three-point formation, hissing and glaring. The milky tan eggs on their eating platter continued to hatch, and the pink fuzzy hatchlings chose that moment to escape.

Lowie let out a stone-rumbling Wookiee roar, and Em Teedee squeaked with a high-pitched alarm. "I can't see a thing, Master Lowbacca! Comestibles are obscuring my optical sensors. Do please clean them off!"

Artoo-Detoo trundled into the dining chamber and let out an electronic wail, but his droid cries were drowned out by the laughter and the tumult of flying food. Before Artoo could wheel around and sound the alarm, a large tray of creamy dessert pastries splattered across his domed top. The astromech droid beat a hasty, whirring retreat.

As the crystal snake slithered toward the cracked stone walls to escape, Jacen desperately plowed forward. He reached out with one hand and grabbed the pointed tail. The serpent rippled around invisibly in a fluid motion, flashing its fangs toward Jacen, ready to bite down on the hand holding it. But Jacen held out his other hand, pointing with his finger and the Force, touching the snake's tiny brain.

"Hey! Don't you dare." he said aloud. Then, as the crystal snake hesitated, Jacen grabbed it around the neck and lifted it into the air.

The lower part of its long body whipped and thrashed. Jacen coiled the snake around his arm and sent soothing thoughts into its mind. He stood up, grinning and relieved.

"I got it!" he cried in triumph—just as three overripe fruits splashed against his face and chest, bursting their thin skins and spilling rich purple pulp all over him. Jacen sputtered and then allowed himself to giggle, still maintaining his hold on the crystal snake.

"Stop!" A booming voice enhanced by the Force echoed through the dining hall.

Suddenly everything froze as if time itself had paused. All the flying food hung suspended in the air; each drip of liquid dangled motionless above the tables. All sound ceased, save for that of the trainees' gasps.

Master Luke Skywalker stood in the entrance to the dining hall wearing a stern expression as he surveyed the suspended food fight. Jacen looked at his uncle's expression and thought he saw anger, but also a concealed amusement.

Luke said, "Was this the best and most challenging way you could find to put your powers to use?" He gestured to all the motionless food and seemed very sad for a moment. Then he turned to leave—but not before Jacen noticed a smile spreading across his face.

As he departed, Luke called, "Instead, perhaps you can use your Jedi powers . . . to clean up this mess." He gestured briefly with his right hand, and the suspended food platters, bowls of soup, desserts, fruits, and messy confections were released, tumbling down like an avalanche. Practically everyone was splattered all over again as sticky gobbets sprayed into the air.

Jacen looked at the aftermath of the food war. Still holding the crystal snake, he wiped a smear of frosting from his nose.

The other Jedi students, though subdued, began to chuckle with relief, then set to work cleaning up.

# 6

THE WARM AFTERNOON sun sparkled in the heavy, moist air as Lowbacca accompanied his uncle and Han Solo back to the *Millennium Falcon*. Beside him the Solo twins chattered gaily, apparently oblivious to the thick jungle heat. He could sense an underlying tension, though: Jacen and Jaina would miss their father every bit as much as he would miss his uncle Chewbacca, his mother, and the rest of his family back on Kashyyyk.

Lowbacca's golden eyes flicked uneasily about the clearing in front of the Great Temple. He was still uncomfortable with wide-open spaces so close to the ground. On the Wookiee homeworld all cities were built high in the tops of the massive intertwining trees, supported by sturdy branches. Even the most courageous of Wookiees seldom ventured to the inhospitable lower levels of the forest—much less all the way to the ground, where dangers abounded.

To Lowbacca, height meant civilization, comfort, safety, home. And although the enormous Massassi trees towered up to twenty times as high as any other plant on Yavin 4, compared with the trees of Kashyyyk they were midgets. Lowbacca wondered if he would ever find a place high enough on this small moon to make him feel at ease.

Lowie was so lost in thought that he was startled to see that they had arrived at the *Falcon*.

"Never have the chance to do a preflight when we're under fire," Han Solo said, "but it's a good idea when we do have the time." Standing at the foot of the entry ramp, he smiled disarmingly at them. "If you kids aren't too busy, Chewie and I could use some help doing the preflight checks."

"Great," Jaina said before anyone else could respond. "I'll take the hyperdrive." She rushed up the ramp, pausing for only a millisecond to brush a kiss on her father's cheek. "Thanks, Dad. You're the best."

Han Solo looked immensely pleased for a long moment before bringing himself back to business with a shake of his head. "So, kid, you got any preferences?" He looked at Lowie, who thought briefly, then rumbled his reply.

Although Han Solo had doubtless understood him very well, the pesky translator droid piped up. "Master Lowbacca wishes to inspect your ship's computer systems in order that he might tell it where to go."

Han Solo gave Chewbacca a sidelong glance. "Thought you said you fixed that thing," he said, indicating Em Teedee. "It needs an attitude adjustment."

Chewbacca shrugged eloquently, gave a menacing growl, and administered emergency repair procedure number one: he held the silvery oval with one huge hand while he shook the little droid until the circuits rattled.

"Oh, dear me! Perhaps I *could* have been a bit more precise," the droid squeaked hastily. "Er . . . Master Lowbacca expresses his desire to perform the preflight checks on your navigational computer."

"Good idea, kid," Han Solo agreed, briskly rubbing his palms together. "Jacen, you take the exterior hull; see if anything's nested in the exterior vents in the last couple of hours. I'll start on the life-support systems. Chewie, you check the cargo bay."

This last was said with a lift of the chin and a twinkle in Han Solo's eye that Lowbacca knew must have meant something to the older Wookiee—but Lowie hadn't a clue. He wondered dispiritedly if he would ever understand humans as well as his uncle did.

The navicomputer was an enjoyable challenge. Lowie ran through all the preflight requirements twice—not because he thought he might have missed something the first time, but because the two places he felt most at home were in the treetops and in front of a computer.

By the time Lowie completed his second run-through, Han Solo had already finished with the life-support systems and was now checking out the ship's emergency power generator. When he saw Lowbacca, Han wiped his hands on a greasy rag, tossed it aside, and held up one finger as if an idea had just come to him. "Why don't you give your uncle a hand in the cargo hold while I finish up here." His roguish grin was even more lopsided than usual.

Lowbacca wondered what the smile meant and why his uncle should still need his help with the cargo. Sometimes humans were very difficult to understand. With a shrug, he headed toward the cargo bay.

"Excuse me, Master Lowbacca," Em Teedee piped up, "but will you be needing my translating services at this time?"

Lowbacca growled a negative.

"Very well, sir," Em Teedee said. "In that

case, would you mind if I put myself into a brief shutdown cycle? If you should require my assistance for any reason, please do not hesitate to interrupt my rest cycle."

Lowie assured Em Teedee that the miniature droid would be the first to know if he needed anything from him.

He found his uncle clambering across a mountain of crates and bundles, checking the securing straps. Apparently Lando Calrissian needed a good many supplies for his new mining operation.

Even in the crowded cargo hold, he breathed deeply, enjoying the mix of familiar smells: speeder fuel, machined metal, lubricants, space rations, and Wookiee sweat—enough to make him homesick for the treetop cities of Kashyyyk. He would have little access to speeders or computers while he studied at the Jedi academy—with the exception, of course, of Em Teedee. But perhaps he could console himself occasionally by climbing the jungle trees and thinking of home.

Maybe he would do that after the *Falcon* took off, but for now there was work to do.

Lowie asked his uncle what still needed to be done, and began to check the webbing on a pile of cargo that Chewbacca indicated. The straps and webbing were loose, and so was the cloth that covered the pile—so loose, in fact, that as Lowbacca began to work, the covering slid away entirely. His jaw dropped, and he stepped back to admire what he had accidentally uncovered.

The air speeder, dismantled into large components, was still recognizable. It was an older model, a T-23 skyhopper, with controls similar to the X-wing fighter, but with trihedral wings, and a passenger seat and cramped cargo compartment at the rear of the cockpit. The blue-metallic hull had been battered and stained with age, but the engine mounted between the wings looked in serviceable condition.

He glanced up to find his uncle staring at him expectantly. Then, to his great surprise, Chewbacca asked Lowie what he thought of the craft.

The skyhopper was compact and well constructed. It wouldn't take much to put all the pieces together again. He complimented the vintage speeder's lines and ventured a guess as to its range and maneuverability. Of course, the onboard computer probably needed a system overhaul and the exterior could use a bit of body work, but those were only minor drawbacks. The dings and scars on the hull only served to add character.

With a satisfied growl, Chewbacca spread his arms wide and shocked Lowie by telling him the T-23 was a going-away gift. The speeder belonged to Lowbacca, if he could assemble it.

Lowbacca stood next to his T-23 in the clearing with Jacen and Jaina and waved good-bye. After a flurry of hugs, exchanged thanks, and last-minute messages, they watched as Han and Chewbacca climbed back aboard the ship.

Now as the *Millennium Falcon* cleared the treetops and angled into the deep blue sky, the three young Jedi trainees continued waving, each lost in thought for a long moment as they gazed after the departing ship.

At last Jaina heaved a sigh. "Well, Lowie," she said, rubbing her hands together with a look of gleeful anticipation as she looked at the battered T-23. "Need any help getting this bucket of bolts up and going?"

Realizing that even though Jaina was younger, she probably had more experience tuning speeder engines than he did, he nodded gratefully.

They spent the next few hours preparing the T-23 for its first flight on Yavin 4. Jacen occupied himself by telling jokes that Lowie didn't understand, or fetching tools for the two enthusiastic mechanics. Jaina smiled as she worked, glad of the rare chance to share what she knew about speeders and engines and T-23s.

When at last they finished and Lowbacca leaned into the cockpit to switch on the engine, the T-23 crackled, sputtered, and roared to life. It lifted off the ground on its lower repulsorlifts, and a bright glow spluttered from the ion afterburners. The three friends let out two cheers and a bellow of triumph.

"Need anyone to take her for a test flight?" Jaina asked hopefully.

Lowie stumbled over a tentative answer. "What Master Lowbacca is trying to say," said Em Teedee, who had long since finished his rest cycle, "is that, as kind as your offer is, he would vastly prefer to pilot the first flight himself."

Lowbacca grunted once.

"And?" the little droid replied. "What do you mean, 'And?' Oh, I see—the other thing you said. But, sir, you didn't mean . . ."

Lowbacca growled emphatically.

"Well, if you insist," Em Teedee said. "*Ahem.* Master Lowbacca also *says* that he would be honored to have you as his passenger, Mistress Jaina. However," he rushed on, "let me assure you that last statement was made with the utmost reluctance."

Lowbacca groaned and hit his forehead with the heel of one hairy hand in a Wookiee expression of complete embarrassment.

"Well, it's certainly the truth," Em Teedee

said defensively. "I'm *certain* I didn't get the intonation wrong."

Jaina, who had at first looked disappointed at Lowbacca's reluctance, now seemed amused at his chagrin. "I understand, Lowie," she said. "I'd want to take her out on my own the first time, too. How about giving us a ride tomorrow?"

Relieved that the twins were not upset, Lowbacca loudly agreed, jumped into the cockpit, and strapped himself in. The whine of the engines drowned out Em Teedee's attempt at translating. Lowie raised a hand in salute, waited until Jacen and Jaina were clear, brought the engines to full power, and took off, heading out toward the vast jungle.

The T-23 maneuvered well, and Lowbacca reveled in the feeling of height and freedom as he streaked away. But still he found himself yearning for one more thing, something that he had been thinking of all day.

The trees. Tall, towering, *safe* trees.

Scarcely half an hour later, far away from the Jedi academy and the Great Temple, he landed the T-23 on the sturdy treetops, settling the craft in the uppermost branches of the Massassi trees. The tree canopy was not as high as he was used to. The air was thinner, and the jungle smells, though not unpleasant, were different from those of

Kashyyyk. Even so, Lowbacca felt more at peace now than he had at any other moment since landing on Yavin 4.

Jacen had said that the huge orange gas giant overhead was best viewed from a Massassi tree—and the human boy was definitely right. Lowie looked around in all directions—at the sky and the trees, at the crumbling ruins of smaller temples visible through breaks in the canopy. He stared at the languid rivers, at the strange vegetation and animals around him. He sighed with relief. He *could* find a place of contentment and solitude on this moon, a place where he could think of family and home while he studied to be a Jedi.

As the late-afternoon sunlight slanted through the thick branches, a distant glint caught Lowbacca's eye. He wondered what it could be. It was not the color of any vegetation or temple ruins. The light reflected from a shiny and evenly shaped object stuck partway up a tree. Lowie leaned forward, as if that could help him see more clearly. He wished he had brought a pair of macrobinoculars.

Curiosity and wonder struck a spark of excitement in him. He wanted to get closer, but caution intervened. It was getting dark. And after all, if the object was important, wouldn't someone have seen it long ago? Perhaps not. He doubted it could be seen from the jungle floor, and it was unlikely that many students came out and climbed to the top of the canopy, this far away from the Great Temple. He was almost certain that no one knew about this discovery.

Heart pounding, Lowie made a mental note of the shiny object's location. He would come back the very first chance he got—he *had* to find out what it was.

# 7

"I WONDER WHY Lowie never made it to
evening meal," Jacen said. Jaina and Tenel
Ka sat next to him in the grand audience
chamber, where Luke Skywalker had summoned them all for a special announcement.
Dusk light shone like burning metal through
the narrow windows overhead, but the clean
white glowpanels dispelled shadows in the
large, echoing room.

"Maybe he was having too much fun flying
his T-23," Jaina whispered. "I probably
wouldn't have made it back either."

"Perhaps," Tenel Ka said in a low voice, as
if giving the matter serious consideration,
"he was not hungry."

Jacen flashed her a look of disbelief. "Hey,
a Wookiee not hungry? Hah! And you say *I*
make dumb jokes."

Tenel Ka shrugged. "It is a thought."

"Okay, well," Jacen said, "I'm not kidding
now—what if something went wrong with

the skyhopper? What if Lowie crashed in the jungle?"

"Impossible," Jaina replied. Though she whispered, her tone was clearly firm. "I checked all those systems myself."

Tenel Ka's eyebrows raised a fraction. "Ah. Ah-hah. So because you checked them, the systems could not malfunction?" She nodded, and Jacen could have sworn that he saw the shadow of a smile lurking at the corners of her lips.

"Never mind—there's Lowie," Jacen said with relief, waving his arms to attract their Wookiee friend's attention.

"See?" Jaina said smugly. "Told you nothing could happen."

Jacen pretended not to notice. "You're just in time," he said as the Wookiee joined them. "Master Skywalker should be here anytime now."

No one really knew why this special twilight meeting had been called, but it was fairly unusual. Everyone who lived, worked, or trained at the Jedi academy had arrived, filling the chamber with a hushed excitement.

Jacen whispered, "Where were you, Lowie?"

Lowbacca responded in a low rumble, quieter than any Jacen had ever heard a Wookiee use. Without warning, Em Teedee announced in a clear metallic voice, "Master

Lowbacca wishes it known that he had a most successful expedition and—" The translator droid cut off in midsentence as Lowbacca clamped a ginger-furred hand over the droid's mouth speaker.

"Shhh!" Jaina hissed.

"Can't you turn it down?" Jacen whispered.

Curious eyes turned to stare at them from every section of the grand audience chamber. Lowbacca hunched down in his seat with a chagrined look that needed no interpreter. He craned his neck forward to stare at the droid clipped to his webbed belt. He issued a series of soft, sharp mutters.

"Oh! Oh, dear me," Em Teedee replied in an enthusiastic though much quieter voice. "I *do* beg your pardon. I did not fully comprehend that you didn't intend to share your discovery with everyone present."

"Discovery?" Jacen said. "What did you—"

But Master Skywalker chose that moment to make his entrance. A hush fell over the crowd, putting an end to all hope of Jacen satisfying his curiosity before the meeting began. Luke mounted the steps to the wide raised platform, closely followed by a slender woman with flowing silvery-white hair and huge opalescent eyes.

"Thank you for gathering here on such short notice," Luke began. "I received news this morning of a pressing matter that calls me away."

As if from a pebble tossed into a pond, a series of surprised murmurs rippled through the room. Jacen wondered if his uncle's imminent departure had anything to do with the messages brought by his father on the *Falcon*.

The blue eyes that looked out over the audience—kind eyes that seemed wise beyond their years—gave no hint of what the Jedi Master's mission might be.

"I don't know how long I will be gone, so I've asked one of my former students, the Jedi Tionne"—he gestured to the slender, shimmering-eyed woman beside him—"to supervise your training while I'm away. Not only does Tionne know my teachings almost as well as I do, but she has a rich knowledge of Jedi lore and history. As you are about to find out, she's well worth listening to."

This intrigued Jacen. He remembered hearing that she was not a particularly strong Jedi, but from the warm smile that passed between Luke and Tionne, he could tell that they understood each other well, and that Master Skywalker must have complete trust in his former student.

As Luke withdrew from the platform, leaving the students alone with Tionne, the silver-haired Jedi retrieved a curiously shaped stringed instrument from somewhere behind her. It consisted of two resonating boxes, one at either end of a slender fretted neck. The strings stretching across the instrument flared out in a fan pattern at both ends.

Seating herself on a low stool, Tionne began to strum. "I will tell you about a Jedi Master who lived long ago," she said. "This is the ballad of Master Vodo-Siosk Baas."

As she began to sing, Jacen agreed with his uncle: Tionne was indeed worth listening to. Her song rang clear and true. Its pure tones carried easily to the farthest corners of the great hall and transported them all to a time they had never witnessed. The music flowed around them, sweeping them along on currents of excitement and courage and triumph and sacrifice.

She sang of dire events that had taken place four thousand years earlier—how the strange, alien Jedi Master had been destroyed by Exar Kun, one of his own students who had turned to the dark side. Master Vodo had begged the other Jedi Masters not to do battle with Exar Kun, and had tried to reason with him alone—though his gentle hopes had ended in tragedy.

In the silence that followed her song, a flood of insight washed through Jacen as he realized that this Jedi was worth listening to for more than just her voice.

Tionne stood, to a collective sigh from everyone present. Jacen hadn't even realized he'd been holding his breath.

"I trust my first lesson to you hasn't been too painful," she said with a merry twinkle in her pearly eyes. "Tomorrow I will give another lesson, after morning meal."

With that, the evening meeting ended. Some listeners remained seated, transfixed, as if trying to absorb the last trickles of music lingering in the room. Others left singly or in whispering groups, while still others stayed behind to talk with Tionne.

Jacen, Jaina, Tenel Ka, and Lowbacca found themselves free at last to talk. They huddled together and discussed Lowie's find. Em Teedee—carefully modulating his voice to an appropriate, secretive level—provided translations.

They speculated by turns about the strange glinting object that Lowbacca had seen out in the jungle. They came to only one conclusion: at the earliest possible opportunity, they would go out together and investigate.

Tionne's morning ballad fell in a fine musical mist, drenching its listeners with wonder and ancient lore. Jacen sat in the second row with his brandy-colored eyes closed, concentrating on her words, trying to absorb everything the music had to teach him. It was just as well that his eyes were shut, since his view was completely blocked by the colorful bulk of Raynar wearing his finest robes.

As the last notes drained away, Jacen opened his eyes to find his sister staring at him in silent amusement. Neither Lowbacca nor Tenel Ka, who sat beside him, gave any indication that they had noticed Jacen's apparent absorption in the music. Then Tionne spoke, drawing Jacen's attention back to the silver-haired Jedi on the raised platform.

"A Jedi's greatest power comes not from size or from physical strength," she said. "It comes from understanding the Force—from trusting in the Force. As part of your Jedi training you will learn to build your confidence and belief through practice. Without that practice we may not succeed when it is most important. This is true of many skills in life. Listen to a story.

"Once, a young girl lived by a lake. Simply by watching others, she learned much about how to swim. One day when her family was busy, the girl jumped into the deep water. Although she moved her arms and legs as she had seen other swimmers do, she could not keep her head above the water.

"Fortunately a fisherwoman jumped in and rescued her. The woman, a practiced swimmer, had not needed to think about how to swim, but the little girl—who had only learned by watching—did not have the skill even to stay afloat. After they were safely out of the water, the fisherwoman took the girl's hand and said, 'Come to the shallows, child, and I will teach you to swim.'"

Tionne paused as if lost in thought, her pearly eyes glittering. "So it is with the Force. Unless we practice what we learn, and unless we are tested, we never know we can trust in the Force if the need arises. That is why this Jedi academy is also called a *praxeum*. It is a place where we not only learn, but we put the learning to use. As with swimming, the more we practice, the more confidence we have. Eventually, our skill becomes second nature.

"The next several days I would like the beginning and intermediate students to practice one of the most basic skills: using the Force to lift. For today, practice lifting only something small—no bigger than a leaf."

Raynar interrupted in a blustery voice, "How can you expect us to *strengthen* our skills if you take us back to a child's level?"

Jacen rolled his eyes at Raynar's rudeness, but he had to admit that he had been wondering the same thing.

Tionne smiled down at Raynar without annoyance. "A good question. Let me give you an example. If you wanted to strengthen your arms, you might lift many stones one time, or you might lift one stone many times. It is the same with your Jedi skills. For today, practice just as I have asked you. It is not the *only* way to strengthen your skills, but it is *one* way. There are always alternatives. I promise you will learn more than just how to lift a leaf."

Tionne dismissed the students. As they left the grand audience chamber and started down the worn stone stairs, Jaina pulled the other three young Jedi to a halt, her eyes dancing. "Are you thinking what I'm thinking?" she asked.

Jacen, who did not know what she was thinking, nonetheless sensed her excitement and her eagerness to investigate Lowie's mysterious discovery.

Jaina shrugged. "What better place to practice lifting leaves than out in a jungle?"

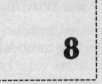

# 8

"YOU SURE THIS seat is safe?" Jacen asked as he squeezed himself into the cargo well behind the T-23's passenger seat.

"Of course it is," his sister replied automatically as she climbed into the front. "You like crawling into cramped spaces anyway."

"Only to catch bugs," he grumbled. "There's no cushioning back here."

The cargo well was much too small to accommodate Tenel Ka, who was taller and more solidly built than either of the twins. Jacen would have to settle for the back or be left behind; his sister would take her turn there on the return trip. He squirmed and settled in as the T-23's engines started with a roaring purr.

Lowie called a command over the sound of the warming repulsorlifts. Em Teedee said, "Master Lowbacca requests that you please be certain that your restraints are secure. He is interested in your utmost safety. We shall be departing momentarily."

Lowbacca's voice barked out again, and the droid amended his translation. "Actually, Master Lowbacca *might* have said something closer to, 'Hold on, everyone. Here we go!'"

"Oh, blaster bolts. No crash straps either," Jacen observed as Jaina and Tenel Ka buckled themselves in up front.

The rebuilt T-23 lifted off with a small jerk. The wind howled past the rattling window plates as they picked up height and speed. Jacen felt the thrill of being airborne as the ion afterburners spluttered behind them. Even cramped in the back, he was glad he hadn't stayed behind.

Jacen looked out through the scratched port as Lowbacca let the skyhopper skim just above the treetops, arrowing away from the Jedi academy into unexplored territory. Soon there were nothing but trees as far as Jacen could see through the scratched port, as lush and green as the sky above him was blue.

Though he enjoyed the lovely foliage below him, Jacen's legs began to cramp. By the time the T-23 dove down and came to rest in a small clearing, he could feel the engine vibrations all the way to his teeth.

Up front, Jaina and Tenel Ka unbuckled their restraints and scrambled nimbly out of the T-23. Jacen dragged himself from the cargo well, stretching his stiff legs as he stepped out into the tangled underbrush. He rubbed the seat of his jumpsuit with both hands to get the circulation going again. "I think a leaf is about all I *could* lift right now!"

Lowie rushed to the edge of the clearing, beckoning the others. "Master Lowbacca says the tree holding the artifact is over here," Em Teedee called. "It has several broken branches, so he was able to locate it easily from the air."

Jaina looked in the direction that Lowbacca was pointing. "Well, what are we waiting for?" she said. Tenel Ka marched over to the young Wookiee, as if ready to carve a path through the jungle. Jacen took a long and wistful look at all the strange new plants he saw around him, but followed the others into the deep green shadows.

Lowbacca gestured up into the distant branches of an enormous Massassi tree. The trunk seemed as big around as one of the skyscrapers on city-covered Coruscant, and even the lowest branches were well out of Jacen's reach. But Lowie wanted them to climb up after him!

"Oh," said Jaina, a crestfallen look on her face, "I wouldn't get very far climbing that."

Lowbacca assured them, via Em Teedee, that the climb would be easy for a Wookiee. He offered to go up alone for the first investigation and report his findings so they could decide the next step.

"We can explore down here," Jacen suggested. "We might find some other pieces of . . . of whatever it is." *Or maybe some interesting animals or fungus or insects,* he thought hopefully.

Jaina and Tenel Ka readily agreed. Lowbacca swiped a hairy hand along the thick black streak that ran through the fur above his left eyebrow. He swarmed up the trunk, swung into the lower branches, and soon disappeared from sight.

Jacen's stomach rumbled with hunger, and he hoped that Lowbacca would hurry. The three young Jedi trainees poked around in the underbrush, spiraling out from the T-23 in a wandering search pattern. Taking turns, they practiced their leaf-lifting assignment, fluttering leaves in the shrubbery, lifting dry forest debris from the damp and mossy ground.

Before long, Lowbacca came crashing back down through the thick branches. He dropped to the ground near them and let out a loud Wookiee cry.

Jaina ran toward him, eager and interested. "Did you find it, Lowie?"

Lowbacca nodded vigorously.

"What was it?" Jaina asked. "Can you describe it?"

"Master Lowbacca believes it to be some sort of solar panel," Em Teedee translated as the Wookiee replied. Then the droid launched into a complete description.

Jaina felt her skin prickle with goose bumps. "Hmmmm," she said. "If I'm right, there should be a lot more to that artifact than what Lowie saw. Let's keep looking."

Tenel Ka dug into a small supply pouch she carried with her and withdrew a pack of carbo-protein biscuits. "Here. Nourishment as we search."

Jacen chomped hungrily on his biscuit. "Just what are we looking for, Jaina?" he asked, speaking around a mouthful of crumbs.

"Scrap metal, machinery, another solar panel." Jaina shaded her eyes, scanning deeper into the thick jungles around them. "We'll keep widening the circle of our search until we find something. What we're looking for shouldn't be too far away."

Jacen retrieved a flask of water from the T-23, took a gulp, and handed it to his sister. Jaina took a few mouthfuls of water and passed the flask on to Lowbacca. Then she set off at a trot for the base of the big tree. Jaina didn't look back to see if the others were following, and bit her lip, feeling a brief pang of guilt.

At times like this Jaina always seemed to assume leadership, just like her mother. But how could she help it? Her parents had raised all three of their children to assess a situation, weigh the alternatives, and make decisions.

"Let's spread out," she said.

"Great!" Jacen said, walking around the massive trunk toward a clump of dense undergrowth.

Jaina smiled, knowing full well that her brother's excitement came not from a desire to find the mysterious artifact, but from the opportunity to explore the jungle and examine its creatures more closely.

She was about to head into the underbrush herself when Lowbacca stopped her with a questioning growl. Em Teedee translated. "Master Lowbacca says—and I personally am inclined to agree with him—that the jungle floor is *not* a safe place to split up. Even to speed up a search."

As impatient as she was to continue looking, Jaina stopped to consider. Tenel Ka caught her eye, placed her hands on her hips, and nodded. "This is a fact."

Jaina gnawed at her lower lip again, thinking, and came to a decision. "All right. We spread out a little bit, but only as far as our line of sight. Good enough?"

The others' murmurs of agreement were

interrupted by a loud squawking as a flock of reptile birds took flight from the bushes near where Jacen had been exploring. Jacen emerged from the bushes on his hands and knees, looking startled, but not displeased.

"No big discoveries," he reported, "but I did find this." He held out his palm. In it was a plump, furry gray creature, quivering in a small nest of glossy fibers.

Another animal. Jaina sighed with resignation. She might have guessed.

"Ah. A-hah," Tenel Ka said. Lowbacca bent forward to run a shaggy finger along the tiny creature's back.

"Look, Jaina," Jacen said, turning the fluffy nest in his hand. He pointed to a dull, flat loop of metal that was firmly attached to the mass of fibers.

"A . . . buckle?" Jaina said, finally comprehending.

Her brother nodded. "Like the kind in crash webbing."

"Good work," Tenel Ka said with solemn approval.

"Well, what are we waiting for?" Jaina asked. "Let's keep going."

By midafternoon, though, Jaina began to get discouraged. Jacen, on the other hand, was intrigued by every crawling creature or insect they encountered.

"Do please try to be a bit more cautious!"

Jaina could hear Em Teedee saying. "That's the third dent today. And I've lost count of how many scratches I've received while you've been exploring. Now if you would only be more attentive to—"

Em Teedee's admonishments were drowned out as Lowie gave a sharp bark of surprise behind a tangle of vines and branches. "Oh! Oh, my. Mistress Jaina, Master Jacen, Mistress Tenel Ka!" Em Teedee's voice was loud enough to startle not only Jaina but a number of flying and climbing creatures. "Do come quickly. Master Lowbacca has made a discovery."

Needing no further encouragement, all of them rushed to see what Lowbacca had found. Jaina felt her heart pounding in her chest, knowing and dreading what they would find.

They worked quickly, scratching and cutting their hands as they pulled away the thick plant growth from the heap of metallic wreckage. Jaina gasped as they finally exposed it—a rounded, tarnished cockpit large enough only for a single pilot, one squarish black solar panel crisscrossed with support braces. The other panel was missing, stuck up in the tree where Lowie had found it. But still the ship was unmistakable.

A crashed Imperial TIE fighter.

# 9

"BUT WHY WOULD such a craft be here in the jungles of Yavin 4?" Tenel Ka asked, narrowing her eyes in concern as they worked to remove the debris from the ruined craft. "Is it an Imperial spy ship?"

Jaina shook her head. "Can't be. TIE fighters were short-range ships used by the Empire. They weren't equipped with hyperdrive, so there aren't many ways it could have gotten here."

Jacen cleared his throat. "Well, I *can* think of one way," he said, "but that would make this ship—let's see . . ."

"Over twenty years old . . ." Jaina breathed, finishing his sentence for him.

Lowbacca made a low, questioning noise, and Tenel Ka continued to look perplexed.

Jaina explained. "When the Empire built the first Death Star, it was the most powerful weapon ever made. They tested it by destroying Alderaan, our mother's homeworld. Then they brought it here to Yavin 4, to destroy the Rebel base."

As she spoke, Jaina pulled the last bit of brush away from the top canopy of the TIE fighter and looked inside. There were no bones. She slid into the musty cockpit.

"A lot of Rebel pilots died in one-on-one combat with the TIE fighters that protected the Death Star, and a lot of Imperial fighters were shot down too," Jacen said, picking up the story.

Jaina wrinkled her nose at the mildewy smell, the mold-clogged controls. She ran her fingers over the navigation panels in the cockpit, closing her eyes and wondering what it must have been like twenty-some years ago to be a fighter pilot in the Battle of Yavin 4. She envisioned an enemy fighter swooping toward her in a strafing run, her engine hit, her tiny ship careening out of control. . . .

Jacen's voice broke into her thoughts. "But then in the end, our dad flew cover for Uncle Luke's X-wing fighter while he took his final run. Uncle Luke made the shot that blew up the Death Star."

Tenel Ka nodded gravely, her braided red-gold hair like a wreath around her head. "And why is it called a TIE fighter?" she asked.

Jaina answered, speaking up from the

cockpit, "Because it has twin ion engines. T-I-E, see?"

Ducking her head, she wormed her way to the engine access panels at the rear of the cockpit and pried open the tarnished metal plate. A squeaking rodent, disturbed from its hidden nest, scampered away, vanishing through a small hole in the hull.

Jaina tinkered with the engines, checking integrity, noting the rotted hoses and fuel lines. But overall, the primary motivators seemed intact, though she would have to run numerous diagnostics. She had plenty of spare parts in her room.

She stood up slowly in the cockpit and poked her head out again, then ran her callused hands along the side of the crashed TIE fighter. "You know, I think we could do it," Jaina said.

All eyes turned toward her, questioning.

"I think we could fix the TIE fighter."

Her brother stared at her in stunned silence for a moment, then clapped a palm to his forehead. "I've got a bad feeling about this."

As the whine of the T-23 skyhopper faded into the jungle distance, the frightened forest creatures settled back into their routines. They scuttled through the underbrush, chasing each other across the branches, predator and prey. The leaves stirred and flying creatures sent their cries from treetop to treetop, forgetting the intruders entirely.

Far below on the forest floor, the branches of a dense thicket parted. A worn and tattered black glove pushed a thorny twig aside.

The pilot of the crashed TIE fighter emerged from his hiding place into the newly trampled clearing.

"Surrender is betrayal," he muttered to himself, as he had done so many times before. It had become a litany during his years of rugged survival on the isolated jungle moon of Yavin.

The pilot's protective uniform hung in rags from his gaunt frame, worn to tatters and patched with furs from an incredible number of years living alone in the jungle. His left arm, injured during the crash, was drawn up like a twisted claw against his chest. He stepped forward, cracking twigs under his old boots as he made his way to the crash site that was no longer secret. He had camouflaged the wrecked Imperial craft many years ago, hiding it from Rebel eyes. But now, despite all his work, it had been discovered.

"Surrender is betrayal," he said again. He stared down at his fighter, trying to see what damage the Rebel spies had caused.

# 10

OVER THE NEXT few days, Tionne increased the complexity of the young Jedi trainees' assignments, and the four companions practiced fine-tuning their control of the Force.

Jaina, Jacen, Lowie, and Tenel Ka found excuses to return again and again to the site of the crashed TIE fighter. With Jaina as the driving force, they took on the repair project as a group exercise—but they always managed to work in any assigned practice sessions during their jungle expeditions.

Although the idea was not flattering, Jaina was forced to admit that part of her motivation for this work was her envy of Lowbacca's personal T-23—she wanted her own craft to fly over the treetops. But she was also drawn by the challenge the wrecked TIE fighter represented. Its age and complexity offered a unique opportunity for learning about mechanics, and Jaina could not turn it down.

But the strongest reason for taking on the project—and perhaps the one that kept them all working without complaint—was that it forged a bond among the four friends. They learned to function as a team, to make the most of each person's strengths and to compensate for each other's weaknesses. The strands of their friendships intertwined and wove together in a pattern as simple as it was strong. This bond included even Em Teedee, who learned to make verbal contributions at appropriate times and was gradually accepted as a member of their group.

Jaina spent most of her time overseeing the mechanical repairs, while Lowbacca concentrated on the computer systems. Jacen had ample opportunity to explore and to observe the local wildlife as, officially, he "searched" through the nearby underbrush for broken or missing components; he also made quick supply trips back to the academy in the T-23 for parts that Jaina or Lowbacca needed. Tenel Ka worked with quiet competence on any task that needed doing and was especially valuable in lugging new metal plates to patch large breaches in the TIE hull.

"Hey, Tenel Ka!" Jacen said. "What goes ha-ha-ha . . . *thump!*"

Her gray eyes looked at him, as lustrous as highly polished stones. "I don't know."

"A droid laughing its head off!" Jacen said, then started giggling.

"Ah. A-hah," Tenel Ka said. She considered this for a moment, then added without the slightest trace of mirth, "Yes, that is very funny." She bent back to her work.

From time to time Lowie climbed to the top of the canopy to meditate and absorb the solitude; the young Wookiee enjoyed his time alone, sitting in silence. Tenel Ka occasionally took short breaks to test her athletic skills by running through jungle undergrowth or climbing trees.

But Jaina preferred to stay with the downed TIE fighter, examining it from every angle and imagining possibilities. She considered no bodily position too difficult or undignified to assume while repairing the craft.

Jaina tucked her head under the cockpit control panel, with her stomach supported by the back of the pilot's seat. Her backside was sticking high in the air and her feet were kicking as she worked, when she felt a playful poke on the leg.

She extricated herself from the awkward position. Lowie handed her a datapad into which he had downloaded the schematics and specifications for a TIE fighter, taken from the main information files in the computer center back at the Great Temple. Jaina studied the data and looked over the list of computer parts Lowbacca needed.

"These should be pretty easy for Jacen to find," she said. "I have most of them right in my room."

Em Teedee spoke up. "Master Lowbacca wishes to know which systems you intend to concentrate on next."

Jaina's brow furrowed in judicious concentration. "We've already decided we won't be needing the weapons systems. I think the laser cannons work fine, but I don't intend to hook them up. I suppose the next step might be to work on the power systems. I haven't done much with them yet."

Jacen and Tenel Ka trotted up to join the discussion. "You will need the other solar panel," Tenel Ka said. "Up in the tree."

Jacen cocked an eyebrow at her, using Tenel Ka's own phrase. "This is a fact?" Tenel Ka did not smile, but nodded her approval.

Jacen folded his arms across his chest and looked pleased with himself. "Does anyone remember the assignment Tionne gave us for today?"

"Cooperative lifting with one or more other students," Tenel Ka stated without hesitation.

Jaina clapped her hands and rubbed them together, scrambling out of the cramped cockpit. "Well, then, what are we waiting for?"

The process was much more difficult than they had anticipated, but in the end they managed it. Lowie and Tenel Ka climbed up into the tree to clear away the moss and branches that held the panel in place. Tenel Ka secured it with the thin fibercord from her belt, while Lowbacca added sturdy vines to help support the heavy slab. Jaina and Jacen watched from the lower branches of the tree, craning their necks to see.

"Everyone ready?" Jaina asked. "Okay— now concentrate," she said. She gave them a moment to observe the solar panel glittering in scattered light from the sky. They studied the piece of wreckage, grasping it with their thoughts.

"Now," Jaina said.

With that, four minds pushed upward, nudging. In a gentle, concerted motion they lifted the panel free of the branch where it had rested for decades. The large, flat rectangle wobbled in midair for a moment and then began to slowly descend. Tenel Ka kept her fibercord taut, easing the Force-lightened object down.

Together, they brought it to rest a few branches below where it had been. Tenel Ka and Lowbacca untied the vines and the fibercord from the higher branch, climbed down, and retied the strands to the branch on which the panel now rested.

The process was not perfect. Mental coordination among the four friends proved difficult, and they each lost their grip more than once. But the vines and fibercord held, preventing a disaster.

By the time the exhausted companions brought the panel to the jungle floor and carried it to the crash site, all of them were panting and perspiring from the mental exertion.

Jaina sank down beside the TIE fighter with a weary groan. She flopped backward in the dirt and leaves, not caring for the moment that her hair would become as disheveled and full of twigs as her brother's usually was.

Lowie tossed them each a packet of food from the basket of supplies they brought with them every day. Jaina's packet landed on her stomach, and she rolled onto her side with a mock growl of indignation. As she faced a hole in the side of the broken TIE fighter, a sudden thought occurred to her.

"You know," she said, chin in hands. "I'd be willing to bet there's enough room in there to install a hyperdrive."

"You said that TIE fighters were short-range craft," Tenel Ka said.

Lowie responded with a contemplative sound as he thought this over. Jacen merely moaned at the mention of more work.

"They were *designed* to be short-range," Jaina said. "Never equipped with hyperdrives because the Emperor didn't want to sacrifice the maneuverability."

Jacen snorted. "Or maybe he didn't want any of his fighter pilots making a quick escape."

Jaina turned toward him and grinned. "I guess I never thought of it that way." Her face lit with enthusiasm as she looked at her friends. "But there's nothing to stop us from equipping *this* TIE fighter with a hyperdrive, is there? Dad gave me one to tinker with."

"It is a possibility," Tenel Ka said, without much enthusiasm.

They were all tired, Jaina knew. But her mind raced with the excitement of this new thought. She made a quick decision. "Okay, let's go back to the academy. I want to make some measurements. We'll call it a day."

Jacen sighed with relief. "I think that's been your best suggestion in hours."

Back again the next afternoon, Jacen lay flat on his stomach, his chin resting on one clenched fist as he surveyed the moist ground beneath a tangle of low, thick bushes. He left his feet sticking out from beneath the bushes

so that the others could locate him easily
should they look up from their work—
though there was little chance of that. From
behind him he could hear thumping and
clinking as Jaina labored to install the hyperdrive in the TIE fighter.

A thick *splat* told him that Tenel Ka and
Lowbacca were applying sealant over the
hole patch at the base of the reattached solar
panel. The others were all busy, leaving Jacen
free to hunt for "missing parts" again.

He watched, fascinated, as a leaf-shaped
creature that matched the blue-green color of
the foliage around him attached itself to a
branch. It extended a long mottled brown
tongue that flattened against the twig in a
perfect camouflage. Jacen could sense the
leaf creature's anticipation. Soon a crowd of
minute insects, drawn by a smell Jacen could
not discern, landed on the "branch" and
became stuck fast. Jacen chuckled and shook
his head as the leaf creature retracted its
tongue with an audible *fwoookt*.

With nothing interesting to be seen on the
ground, he gave the bush a small shake once
the leaf creature departed. He was rewarded
with a hissing rustle as a dislodged object fell
near his elbow. He picked it up.

It was an Imperial insignia.

He turned the metallic object over in his
hand, but then he saw a familiar shimmer at

the edge of his gaze, and he reflexively grabbed for it. Jacen wriggled backward out of the bushes, stood, and bounded over to the TIE fighter.

"Look what I found!" he crowed. His sister's lower half protruded at an awkward angle from the cockpit, while she was apparently attempting to connect some part of the hyperdrive behind the pilot's seat.

Her muffled voice drifted out to him. "Just a moment. I need a flash heater."

Tenel Ka passed a small tool in from the other side of the open cockpit. She and Lowbacca, wiping sealant from their hands, came around to see what Jacen had discovered.

"A brooch of some sort?" Tenel Ka asked, examining it closely.

Jacen shook his head. "An Imperial insignia. Came off a uniform of some kind."

"There," Jaina said, extracting herself from the cockpit of the TIE fighter and jumping down beside them. "That should do it."

Jacen handed her the insignia, and she nodded absently. "Look what else I found," he said, holding up his left arm, which was wrapped in a glowing shimmer.

Jaina made a sound somewhere between a growl and a laugh, and backed away. "Great. Just what we need—another crystal snake that can get loose."

Jacen used a tactic he knew his sister couldn't resist. "Oh," he said, letting disappointment show. "It's just that you've always been so *good* at designing things—I thought you could come up with a cage that the snakes couldn't escape from. But if you really don't think you can . . ."

He saw Jaina's face light at the challenge, but then her brandy-brown eyes narrowed shrewdly, and he knew that she had caught on. "That," she said, "is a dirty trick. You *know* I could—" She shook her head, sighed in mock exasperation, and seemed to resign herself to the inevitable. "Oh, all right! I'll build you a new cage for your crystal snakes—"

"Thanks," a grinning Jacen cut her off before she could change her mind. "You're the best sister in the whole galaxy!"

Jaina huffed indelicately. "But don't bring this new snake back to your quarters until I have the cage ready."

"Okay," Jacen said, "I'll keep it someplace safe—maybe in the cargo compartment. Can I have the Imperial insignia back, please?" Jaina tossed it to him, and he began to polish it against the sleeve of his jumpsuit. "I wonder if it belonged to the pilot."

Lowbacca looked at the crashed TIE fighter and then back at Jacen and rumbled a question. "Master Lowbacca suggests it is unlikely that the pilot survived the crash, even if his fall was cushioned by the Massassi trees," Em Teedee said.

Tenel Ka looked around the site with unblinking eyes. "No bones."

Jacen shrugged. "After twenty years, that's not surprising. Lots of scavengers in the jungle. I've been assuming he was thrown clear."

Tenel Ka's cool eyes looked troubled, but she nodded. "Perhaps."

The four worked in companionable silence as they attached the final hole patch to the damaged hull. Then, while the other three applied the slow-drying sealant, Jacen hunted around in the underbrush. He knew he shouldn't be out of sight for more than a few seconds, but he had already searched all of the thickets in clear view of the crash site.

Promising himself that he wouldn't be gone long, Jacen pushed through a particularly thick tangle of dense, dark-leaved plants and emerged into a small clearing no wider than his outstretched arms. The dirt was completely devoid of plant life, as if some animal trampled it so often that vegetation no longer grew there. It extended deeper into the jungle—a path! It was narrow, but the hard-packed trail was unmistakable.

Forgetting his earlier promise to stay close, Jacen plunged through the bushes and followed the trail. The grove of Massassi trees was younger, their branches lower to the ground. Perhaps that was why none of the companions had seen this path from up above.

The jungle grew darker around him as he trudged on. The chitters, growls, and screeches of forest animals seemed more menacing.

Just as he began to realize that he was much too far away from the others, he came upon a clearing beside a small stream.

Some creature had built a dam across the stream, diverting some of the water into a depression beside it to form a wide, shallow pool. Against the burn-hollowed trunk of a huge Massassi tree at the water's edge leaned a number of long, fat branches covered with moss and ferns to form a crude shelter—perhaps the lair of the creature whose path Jacen had been following.

Jacen reached out toward the little hovel with his mind, but sensed nothing larger than insects living around it. Skirting the small pond, he approached the low shelter, his heart pounding loudly in his chest. He knew he should be more cautious. But what was this place?

What if the beast that lived here was a predator? What if it returned as he was investigating?

Jacen jumped as he heard a loud *crack*—but it was only a twig snapping under his own foot. He bent forward to look into the branchy opening of the shelter, and gasped at what he saw there.

Fully a third of the Massassi tree's trunk had been hollowed out to form a sturdy, dry cave, tall enough for a man to stand in. A makeshift wooden chair stood beside a low mound of leaves that might have been a bed, partially covered by a ragged piece of cloth. A cache of equipment, vines, fruits, and dried berries lay piled against the back of the cave. Perched atop the pile was a nightmarish black helmet with triangular eyeplates and a breathing mask connected to a pair of rubber hoses that Jacen figured had once been linked with an air tank.

An Imperial TIE fighter pilot's helmet.

Jacen stumbled backward, away from the shelter, his breath coming in shallow gasps. He tripped and fell, and found himself inside a ring of low stones and ashes. A fire pit. He scooped away some of the dirt that covered the pit and felt around with trembling fingers. The ground was still warm.

Jacen jumped to his feet and raced toward the little trail at full speed. He ran along the narrow path, heedless of the branches that slapped his face or the thorns that tore at his jumpsuit, oblivious to the animals he startled from their hiding places. He didn't slow as he approached the bushes that surrounded the crashed TIE fighter.

He burst into the tiny clearing and ran up to the wreck, yelling, "Jaina! Tenel Ka! Lowie! He's here. He's alive. The TIE pilot isn't dead!"

The three of them looked up in astonishment just as Jacen heard a rustling in the bushes behind him. He turned to see a haggard, grizzled-looking man step through the bushes. The stranger's face was deeply lined, and he wore a tattered flight suit. His left arm was bent at an awkward angle, and was wrapped in an armored gauntlet of black leather. But in his glove he held an ugly, old-model blaster. And the weapon was leveled directly at the young Jedi Knights.

"Yes," said the Imperial fighter pilot. "I am very much alive. And you are my prisoners."

# 11

WHEN THE IMPERIAL TIE pilot turned his eyes from her for a split second, Tenel Ka reacted with lightning speed, just as she had been taught by the warrior women on Dathomir.

"Run!" she shouted to the others, knowing exactly what to do. She turned and bolted for the nearest tangled undergrowth, dodging expected blaster fire.

Tenel Ka reacted so quickly and so smoothly that even her most rigid battle trainers would have been proud of her. Their tactics had been drilled into her:

*Confuse the enemy.*

*Do the unexpected.*

*Take your opponent by surprise.*

*Don't waste time hesitating.*

Tenel Ka tore through the tangled thorns and blueleaf shrubs, clawing with her hands to clear a path that closed behind her as she moved through the thicket. She gasped and panted, bolting ahead, ignoring the scratches and stinging pain of the thorns against her bare arms and legs. The scaled armor protected her vital parts, but her red-gold hair flew around her, snagging loose leaves and twigs. Branches caught at her braids and yanked strands of her hair out by the roots. She hissed with pain, but clamped her teeth together, plunging ahead.

Why couldn't she hear the others running? "Get help!" It was Jacen shouting behind her, still in the clearing. Why didn't they run?

Then an explosion of flames ripped into the underbrush just to her left. The TIE pilot was firing his blaster at her! The smell of singed leaves and burnt sap stung her nostrils. Tenel Ka dove to the ground, rolled sideways, then ran at full speed in a different direction. If she gave up now, he would kill her. She had no doubt of that—not anymore.

Intent only on distancing herself from the TIE pilot, she fled, changing directions at random to confuse the enemy. Branches cracked underfoot, and Tenel Ka paid no attention whatsoever to where she ran . . . deeper into the densest jungle of Yavin 4.

Lowbacca hesitated only a fraction of a second longer.

Tenel Ka seemed to evaporate as she

shouted "Run!" and ducked into the thick forest.

The TIE pilot whirled and pointed his blaster at the place where Tenel Ka had disappeared, and Lowbacca used the instant of distraction. The young Wookiee let out a bellow of surprise and anger, then instinctively surged up the ancient bole of the nearest Massassi tree, climbing higher, *up*, where it was safe.

He grabbed branches and vines, hauling himself up toward the thick, spicy-smelling canopy. Behind him, the Imperial fighter began shooting wildly. Explosions and bright flames from burning foliage ballooned out from where the blaster bolts struck the branches under Lowie's feet. He smelled the ozone of energy discharge, the steam of disintegrated vegetation.

With Wookiee strength, Lowbacca climbed higher and higher, finally reaching thick, flat branches that allowed him to make his way across the treetops toward where he had landed the T-23.

He had to get help. He had to rescue his friends. Tenel Ka had gotten to safety—or so he hoped—but Jacen and Jaina had not been able to react as quickly or move with such practiced wilderness skills.

"Oh my!" Em Teedee wailed from the clip on his waist. "Where are we going? That person was trying to kill us! Can you imagine that?"

Lowie continued to scramble across the thick branches, loping with great agility, moving farther away from the still-firing pilot.

"Master Lowbacca, answer me!" Em Teedee said, his tinny voice echoing from the speaker-patch. "You can't simply leave me hanging here doing nothing at all, you know."

Lowbacca grunted a reply and kept moving.

"But surely, that's beside the point," Em Teedee quibbled, "since I'm doing everything I can. Just because I have no functional arms or legs doesn't mean I don't *want* to assist you."

The sounds of blaster fire from the clearing below had ceased, and Lowbacca feared that meant Jacen and Jaina were captured—or worse. His thoughts churned it in panic and turmoil. He knew he had to rescue them. But how? He had never done anything like this before. He didn't think Tenel Ka could do it alone, so he had to offer whatever help he could manage.

The branches thinned up ahead, spreading out around the clearing where Lowbacca had settled the T-23. The small ship sat where he had landed it, and he scrambled back down the thick branches, clinging to vines until he reached ground level again. The T-23 was his best chance.

Lowbacca had been so proud of the small craft when his uncle Chewie had given it to him, but now it seemed so small and battered, all but useless against an armed Imperial pilot. He trudged across the weed-covered ground over to the little skyhopper. He would have to use it to make the rescue. He had no better options.

The low, simmering music of insects and jungle creatures filled the air. He could hear no sound of blaster fire, no shouts of challenge or pain. It was quiet. Too quiet. Lowbacca hurried.

"Oh, excellent idea!" Em Teedee said as they approached the T-23. "We're going back to the Jedi academy to get reinforcements, aren't we. That's by far the wisest thing to do, I'm sure."

But Lowie knew it would be too late for the twins by then. He had to do something *now*. He told Em Teedee what he intended to do, and the miniature translating droid squawked in dismay.

"But, Master Lowbacca! The T-23 has no weapons. How can you fly it against that Imperial pilot? He is a professional fighter— and he's desperate!"

Lowie had the same fears as he powered up the T-23's repulsorlift engines. He made an optimistic comment to the translating droid.

"Tricks? What tricks do you have up your sleeve?" Em Teedee said. "Besides, you don't even *have* sleeves."

The craft sounded strong and powerful, thrumming and roaring in the jungle stillness. Lowie smelled the acrid exhaust, and snuffled. His black pilot seat vibrated as the ship prepared to take off.

He would need to do some fancy flying to get the craft through the trees to the crash site—but he had to save his friends, offer whatever help he could. Perhaps his noisy approach would startle the TIE pilot enough to make him flee for cover. And then the twins could jump aboard and make their escape.

Lowbacca nudged the throttles forward and lifted the T-23 off its resting place in the trampled undergrowth. The ion afterburners roared as the small ship arrowed through the forest, dodging branches and hanging moss, heading toward his friends—directly into the path of danger.

Back in the clearing, Jacen and Jaina froze for only a moment, then turned and ran, trying to escape—but the bulk of the almost-repaired TIE fighter got in their way. Jaina grabbed Jacen's arm, and the two of them ran together, frightened but knowing they needed to move, *move*.

The Imperial pilot fired his blaster, shooting twice into the thicket where Tenel Ka had vanished. Burning brush and splintered twigs flew into the air in a cloud. For an instant Jaina thought their young friend from Dathomir had been killed—but then she heard more leaves rustling and branches snapping as Tenel Ka continued her desperate flight.

The TIE pilot fired into the trees next, blasting the lower branches—but Lowbacca had gotten away. The twins ran around the end of the wrecked fighter, and suddenly Jacen stumbled over a rectangular box of hydrospanners, cyberfuses, and other tools they had gathered for the repair of the crashed ship—and fell headlong.

Jaina grabbed her brother's arm, trying to yank him to his feet to run again. The ground screeched with an explosion of blaster fire. Three high-energy bolts ricocheted from the age-stained hull of the crashed ship.

Jaina froze, raising her hands in surrender. They couldn't possibly hide fast enough. Jacen climbed to his feet and stood next to his sister, brushing himself off. The TIE pilot took two steps toward them, encased in battered armor and wearing an expression of icy anger.

"Don't move," he said, "or you will die, Rebel scum."

His black pilot armor was scuffed and worn from his long exile in the jungles. The Imperial's crippled left arm was stiff like a droid's, encased in an armored gauntlet of black leather. He had been severely hurt, but it appeared to be an old injury that had long ago healed, though improperly. The pilot was a hard-bitten old warrior. His eyes were haunted as he stared at Jaina.

"You are my prisoners." He motioned with the old-model blaster pistol that was gripped in his twisted, gloved hand.

"Put down the blaster," Jaina said quietly, soothingly, using everything she knew of Jedi persuasion techniques. "You don't need it." Her uncle Luke had told them how Obi-Wan Kenobi had used Jedi mind tricks to scramble the thoughts of weak-minded Imperials.

"Put down the blaster," she said again in a rich, gentle voice.

Jacen knew exactly what his sister was doing. "Put down the blaster," he repeated.

The two of them said it one more time in an echoing, overlapping voice. They tried to send peaceful thoughts, soothing thoughts into the TIE pilot's mind . . . just as Jacen had done to calm his crystal snake.

The TIE pilot shook his grizzled head and

narrowed his haunted eyes. The blaster wavered just a little, dropping down only a notch.

*Why isn't it working?* Jaina thought desperately. "Put down the blaster," she said again, more insistently. But inside the Imperial fighter's mind she ran up against a wall of thoughts so rigid, so black-and-white, so clear-cut, that it seemed like droid programming.

Suddenly the pilot straightened and glared at them through those bleak, haunted eyes. "Surrender is betrayal," he said, like a memorized lesson.

Jacen, seeing their chance slipping away, reached out with his mind and yanked at the weapon with mental brute force.

"Get the blaster!" he whispered. Jaina helped him tug with the Force, reaching for the old weapon in the pilot's grip. But the armored glove was wrapped so tightly around it that the black gauntlet seemed fastened to the blaster handle. The handgrip of the obsolete weapon caught on the glove, and the TIE pilot grabbed it with his other hand, pointing the barrel directly at the twins.

"Stop with your Jedi tricks," he said coldly. "If you continue to resist I will execute you both."

Knowing that the pilot needed only to

depress the firing stud—much more quickly than they could ever mind-wrestle the blaster away from him—Jacen and Jaina let their hands fall to their sides, relaxing and ceasing their struggles.

Just then a buzzing, roaring sound crashed through the canopy above—a wound-up engine noise, growing louder.

"It's Lowie!" Jacen cried.

The T-23 plunged through the branches overhead in a crackling explosion of shattered twigs, plowing toward the crash site at full speed, like a charging bantha.

"What's he trying to do?" Jacen asked, quietly. "He doesn't have any weapons on board!"

"He might distract the pilot," Jaina said. "Give us a chance to escape."

But the armored Imperial soldier stood his ground at the center of the clearing, spreading his legs for balance and assuming a practiced firing stance. He pointed his blaster at the oncoming air speeder, unflinching.

Jaina knew that if the blaster bolt breached the small repulsorlift reactor, the entire vehicle would explode—killing Lowbacca, and perhaps all of them.

Lowbacca brought the T-23 forward as if he meant to ram the TIE pilot. The desperate Imperial soldier aimed at the T-23's engine core and squeezed the firing stud.

"No!" Jaina cried, and *nudged* with her mind at the last instant. Using the Force, she shoved the TIE pilot's arm and knocked his aim off by just a fraction of a degree. The bright blaster bolt screeched out and danced along the metal hull of the repulsorlift pods. The engine casings melted at the side, spilling coolant and fuel. Gray-blue smoke boiled up. The sound of the T-23 became stuttered and sick as its engines faltered.

Lowie pulled up in the pilot's seat, swerving to keep from crashing into the Massassi trees. He could barely fly the badly damaged craft.

"Go, Lowie!" Jacen whispered. "Get out while you can."

"Eject! Before it blows!" Jaina cried.

But Lowbacca somehow managed to gain altitude, spinning around the huge trees and climbing toward the canopy again. His engines smoked, trailing a stream of foul-smelling exhaust that curled the jungle leaves and turned them brown.

"He won't get far," the Imperial pilot said in a raw monotone. "He is as good as dead."

Although the T-23 was out of sight now, far above them in the jungle treetops, Jaina could still hear the engine coughing, failing, and then picking up again as the battered craft limped away. The sounds carried well in the jungle silence. The repulsorlift engine faded in the distance, its ion afterburners popping and sputtering—until finally, there was silence again.

The TIE pilot, his expression still stony, gestured with the blaster pistol. "Come with me, prisoners. If you resist this time, you will die."

# 12

LOWBACCA WRESTLED WITH the T-23, trying to control its erratic flight as it lurched across the treetops.

Thick, knotted smoke trailed in a stuttering plume from his starboard repulsor engine. Lowie risked a quick glance to his right again to assess the damage. No flames, but the situation was grim enough. The late-afternoon air currents were turbulent and threatened to capsize the skyhopper.

The T-23 jolted and dipped. Once, it bounced against some upraised branches, which scraped like long fingernails against the ship's lower foils and bottom hull, but Lowbacca managed to wrench the T-23 back on course. He was a good pilot; he would make it back to the academy and bring help, no matter what it took. He didn't know what had happened to Tenel Ka—if she was all right, or if the TIE pilot had captured her by now as well. For all he knew, Lowbacca was the only hope for rescue for his three friends.

His heart pounded painfully and his eyes stung from the chemical smoke that leaked into the cockpit. He noticed a sour, noxious smell, and his head began to swim.

"Master Lowbacca," Em Teedee said, "my sensors indicate that significant quantities of fumes have entered the cockpit."

Lowbacca gave a growl of annoyance. Did the little droid think that his sharp sense of smell hadn't picked that up?

"Well, no," Em Teedee rushed on, "it may not be dangerous *yet*, but if we begin to lose airspeed, less smoke will be drawn away. The airborne toxins could reach potentially lethal levels"—the droid raised his volume slightly for emphasis—"*even for a Wookiee.*"

The speeder gave a shuddering jolt, scraping against branches again. With grim determination Lowbacca pulled up. The T-23 was even harder to manage now. He wasn't sure how long he could last.

But he *had* to make it. He couldn't leave his friends in danger.

The T-23 shuddered and dipped. Lowbacca wheezed, laboring to pull air into his lungs. As if in response to his effort, the starboard engine coughed and sputtered.

And died.

Using all of his piloting skills, Lowie fought

to steady the craft in its wobbling descent. The thick, deceptively soft-looking canopy rushed up at him, and the T-23 came to a crunching halt in a blizzard of leaves and twigs. Like a wounded avian, it lay nestled on the treetops, its right lower wing buried in the foliage. The left engine still chugged, but smoke billowed up from the damaged engine below, pouring into the cockpit now.

Lowbacca's head reeled with the impact, but he knew he had to get out. He fumbled with his crash restraints, trying to unfasten them. His vision was blurred from the acrid smoke, and he gagged at the stench. Confusion made his fingers clumsy.

Finally, with a burst of determination, he yanked on the straps until, loosened by the crash, they tore away. Two of the restraints came free in his hands, and he wriggled out of the remaining webbing.

Still no flames, Lowbacca noted with relief as he scrambled from the cockpit and distanced himself from the smoking T-23. Lowbacca gasped in deep lungfuls of the fresh, humid air of Yavin 4. As he worked his way across the treetops in the gathering dusk, one knee ached from where it had banged against the controls during the crash.

But he had no time to think about that. His first rescue attempt might have failed, but *he* had not failed yet. There were always options. He had to get back to the academy.

In his hurried scramble through the upper branches, Lowbacca did not notice when Em Teedee's clip broke at his waist.

The tiny droid fell with a thin wail into the forest below.

Dusk deepened into the full darkness of the jungle night. Swarms of nocturnal creatures awakened, beginning to hunt—but still Lowbacca pressed on.

Common sense had forced him to travel below the canopy, descending to a level where all of the branches were of a sufficient length and sturdiness to support him as he transferred his agile bulk from one tree to the next. Sometimes when he began to tire, or when his injured knee threatened to give way beneath him, Lowbacca relied on his powerful arms instead, swinging from branch to branch, using his keen Wookiee night vision in the murky shadows.

But he never stopped to rest. He could rest later.

Right now all of his senses were as finely tuned as a medical droid's laser beam. The pads of his feet and his acute sense of smell helped him to avoid decaying patches or slippery growths on the tree branches as he walked. His sharp hearing could distinguish between the sounds of wind through the leaves and the rustling of nocturnal animals as they stalked the jungle heights. For the most part, he managed to stay clear of them.

Lowbacca did not fear the darkness or the jungle. The jungles of Kashyyyk held far greater dangers—and he had faced those and survived. He remembered playing late-night games in the forest with his cousins and friends: races through the upper trees, jumping and swinging competitions, daring expeditions to the dangerous lower regions to test each other's courage, and the usual rites of passage that marked a Wookiee youth's transition into adulthood.

As he pushed through a dense clump of growth, a twig snagged Lowie's webbed belt, and he yanked it free. The feel of the intricately braided strands beneath his fingers reminded him of the night when he had won his belt, of his dangerous rite of passage.

He remembered. . . .

He felt his heart race with excitement as he descended toward the jungle floor that night long ago. Lowie had been down that far only twice before, when he had attended the rites of other friends, as was customary; there was strength in numbers when they sought to harvest the long, silky strands from the center of the deadly syren plant.

But Lowbacca had chosen to go alone,

preferring to meet the challenge of the voracious syren plant using his own wits rather than borrowed muscles.

The night on Kashyyyk had been cool and dank. The profusion of screeches, chirps, growls, and croaks had been overwhelming. When he'd reached the lowest branches, Lowie had cinched the strap of his knapsack tighter and began his hunt.

With every sense fully alert, Lowbacca had moved stealthily from branch to branch until he caught the alluring scent of a wild syren plant. With sure instinct he'd followed the distinctive odor, feeling a mixture of anticipation and dread, until he squatted on the branch directly above the plant. He leaned over to study his stationary, but incredibly vicious, quarry.

The huge syren blossom consisted of two glossy oval petals of bright yellow, seamed in the center and supported by a mottled, bloody red stalk, twice as thick around as the sturdy tree limb on which Lowbacca sat. From the center of the open blossom spread a tuft of long white glossy fibers that emitted a broad spectrum of pheromones, scents to attract any unwary creature.

The beauty of the gigantic flower was intentionally deceptive, for any creature lured close enough to touch the sensitive inner flesh of the blossom would trigger the plant's lethal reflexes, and the petal jaws would close over the victim and begin its digestive cycle.

Alone, Lowbacca intended to harvest the glittering strands of the plant from the center of the flower—without springing the trap.

Traditionally, a few strong friends would hold the flower open while the young Wookiee scrambled to the treacherous center of the blossom, harvested the lustrous strands of sweetly scented fiber, and quickly made an escape. But even this assistance was no guarantee. Occasionally young Wookiees still lost limbs as the carnivorous plant clamped down on a slow-moving arm or leg.

Performing the task by himself, though, Lowie had needed to be extra careful. He had removed the knapsack from his hairy back and extracted its contents: a face mask, a sturdy rope, a thin cord, and a collapsible vibroblade. He'd placed the mask over his nose and mouth to filter out the syren's seductive scents. He knew that the pheromones could produce an almost overpowering desire to linger or to touch—and he could afford no mistakes.

Working quickly, enveloped by sinister night sounds, he had fashioned a short length of thin cord into a loose slipknot, then formed a loop to make a sort of seat for himself in the sturdy, longer rope. Passing the free end of the long rope over a branch directly above the syren plant, he'd gathered up the slack in one hand, slid off the limb, and lowered himself with muscular arms.

Lowie had positioned himself as close as he dared to the gently undulating petals of the hungry syren blossom, an arm's length from the tantalizing tuft. He'd gripped the end of the long rope in his strong jaws to hold himself in place and free his hands. Then, using the loop of thin cord to lasso the tuft of precious fibers, he'd pulled himself close enough to slice them loose with his vibro-blade. With a triumphant growl he'd jerked his prize toward himself, trapped the bundle against his body with one hairy arm, and stuffed the fiber into his knapsack.

In his excitement, however, the rope had slipped from his teeth. The trailing end uncoiled, dangled precariously, and then brushed one glossy petal of the deadly flower below. With a surge of gut-wrenching terror, Lowbacca had grabbed the tied end of rope and hauled himself upward as the syren's jaws snapped shut. The petals just grazed one foot as they closed with an ominous slurp and a backwash of wind.

He had earned this fiber, Lowie thought, every strand of it, enough to make a special belt, which he always wore afterward.

•    •    •

Exhaustion sank its claws into every muscle as Lowbacca made his way from one Massassi tree to the next, hour after hour, all through the night.

Distance held no more meaning for him; he had to get to the Jedi academy. He could hear nothing but his own ragged breathing. His injured leg wobbled unsteadily at each step. Fatigue blurred his vision, and twigs and leaves matted his fur. He pushed forward, always forward, arm-leg, arm-leg, hand-foot, hand-foot—

Lowie looked around, confused and disoriented. He had reached for the next branch, but there were no more branches. Raising his head, he looked across the clearing—the landing clearing!—and saw the Great Temple, its majestic tiers outlined in the predawn darkness by flickering torches.

Lowbacca never remembered afterward climbing down out of the tree or crossing the clearing. He noticed only the awesome, welcoming sight of the ancient stone pyramid as he bellowed an alarm. He roared again and again, until a stream of robed figures carrying fresh torches rushed out of the temple and down the steps toward him.

The night and the desperate journey had taken their toll on Lowie. The numbness imposed by his own determination had worn off, and his knee refused to hold him any longer. His gangly legs gave way, and he collapsed to the ground, moaning his message.

When he rolled onto his back, a circle of concerned faces filled his vision. Tionne bent over him and brushed the tangle of matted fur away from his eyes.

"Lowbacca, we were concerned for you!" Tionne said gravely. "Are you hurt?"

Lowie groaned an answer, but Tionne didn't seem to understand. She leaned closer to him, her silvery hair glowing in the torchlight.

"Were Jacen and Jaina with you? And Tenel Ka?" She paused as he tried to moan another answer. "Did something happen?" she persisted. "Can you tell me where they are?"

Lowbacca finally managed to say that the others were in the jungle and needed help. Tionne's brows knitted together in an expression of worry. She blinked her mother-of-pearl eyes. "I'm sorry, Lowbacca. I can't understand a word you're saying."

Lowie reached toward his belt to activate Em Teedee—but he found nothing. The translator droid was gone.

# 13

TENEL KA RAN through the cool near-darkness of the jungle floor, trying to come up with a plan. She held her bent arms in front of her to protect her eyes and to push obstacles from her path. Branches whipped her face, tore at her hair, and clawed mercilessly at her bare arms and legs.

Her breath came in sharp gasps, not so much from the effort of running—to which she was well accustomed—but from the terror of what she had just experienced. She hoped she had made the right decision. Her pulse pounded in her ears, competing with the symphony of alien noises as the jungle creatures welcomed nightfall. Though she searched her mind, no Jedi calming techniques would come to her.

When the loud squawk of flying creatures sounded directly behind her, Tenel Ka glanced back in alarm. Before she could turn again, she fetched up sharply against the trunk of a Massassi tree. Stunned, she fell back a few paces and sank to the ground, putting one hand to the side of her face to examine her injury.

*No blood*, she thought as if from a great distance. *Good*. Beneath her fingertips, she felt tenderness and swelling from her cheek to her temple. There would be bruises, of course, and perhaps a royal headache. She cringed at the thought. *Royal*. Although no one could see it, her cheeks heated with a flush of humiliation.

Tenel Ka pulled herself to her feet and took stock of her situation. In her newfound calmness she admitted to herself that she was completely lost. Jacen and Jaina—and by now perhaps even Lowbacca—were counting on her to return with help. She had always prided herself on being strong, loyal, reliable, unswayed by emotion. She had been levelheaded enough during her initial escape, but then she had panicked. She shook off thoughts of her stupid headlong flight.

*Well*, she thought, pressing her pale lips together into a firm line, *I am back in control now*. She decided to push on until she found a safer place to spend the night. When morning came, she would try to get her bearings again and return to the Jedi academy.

As she trudged along, searching in the fading light of day, the ground began to rise and become more rocky. The trees grew sparser. When she saw a jagged shadow loom out of the darkness ahead of her, she slowed. Ahead was a large outcropping of rough, black stone, long-cooled lava mottled with lichens.

Tenel Ka tilted her head back and looked up, but she could not see how high the rock went; the jungle dimness swallowed it up. Cautiously exploring sideways, she encountered a break in the rock face, a patch of deeper darkness—a small cave. Perhaps she could spend the night here, in this defensible, sheltered place. The opening was no wider than the length of one arm and extended only to shoulder height, forcing her to stoop to explore further. She needed only to find a comfortable, safe place to rest.

She shivered as she hunched down on the sandy, cool floor of the cave. Her every muscle ached, but for now nothing could be done about her pain; she could bear it as well as any warrior. But she had not eaten since midday. She felt in the pouch at her waist, finding one carbo-protein biscuit remaining. As for the cold, she could light a fire with the finger-sized flash heater she carried in another pouch on her belt.

Dropping to her hands and knees, she scrabbled along the ground near the mouth of the cave, searching for twigs, leaves, anything that would burn. Back on Dathomir she'd had plenty of practice in rugged camping and outdoor endurance.

As she thought of the cozy warmth of a fire and a soft bed of leaves, Tenel Ka's spirits rose. The nightmarish events of the afternoon began to settle into perspective. This was an adventure, she assured herself. A test of her will and determination.

When she had collected kindling and some thicker branches, Tenel Ka began to build her fire against the velvety shadows of gathering night. She fumbled in her belt pouches for her flash heater and groaned as she remembered that Jaina had borrowed it that afternoon. She rubbed her cold, bare arms and blew on her hands to warm them.

Tenel Ka thought longingly of the cheery warmth of a crackling fire, of drinking hot, spiced Hapan ale with her parents. A rare smile crossed her lips as she thought of them, Teneniel Djo and Prince Isolder. If she were at home, she would only have to lift a hand to bring a servant of the Royal House of Hapes running to do her bidding. . . .

Tenel Ka grimaced. She had never known poverty or hardship, except by choice. *Well, you* chose *this, Princess*, she reminded herself savagely. *You wanted to learn to do things for yourself.*

Her father, Isolder of Hapes, had always

said that the two years he spent in disguise working as a privateer had done more to prepare him for leadership than any training the royal tutors of Hapes could provide. And her mother, raised on the primitive planet of Dathomir, was proud that her only daughter spent months each year learning the ways of the Singing Mountain Clan and dressing as a warrior woman—a practice that Tenel Ka had enjoyed all the more because it annoyed her scheming Hapan grandmother.

Teneniel Djo had been even more pleased when her daughter had decided to attend the academy and take instruction to become a Jedi. She had enrolled simply as Tenel Ka of Dathomir, not wanting the other trainees to treat her differently because of her royal upbringing.

At the academy, only Master Skywalker—who was an old friend of her mother's, and the man Teneniel Djo most admired—knew Tenel Ka's true background. She had not even told Jacen and Jaina, her closest friends on Yavin 4.

Jacen and Jaina. The twins trusted her. They needed her help now. She shivered in the cave. She had to stay safe for the night and then get back to the academy in the morning to bring reinforcements.

Tenel Ka heard a faint rustling, slapping, and hissing in the darkness behind her. She looked back into the undulating shadows, blinking to clear her eyes. Had the shadows really moved? Perhaps she had been foolish to spend the night in an unexplored cave, but cold and fatigue had overruled her natural caution. She looked up and thought she could discern glossy dark shapes clinging to the ceiling, moving like waves on an inverted black sea.

*Don't be a child*, she chided herself. She had always tried to show her friends how self-sufficient and reliable she was. Right now, she was cold and bruised and miserable. What would Jacen say if he could see her? He'd probably tell some dumb joke.

Tenel Ka gritted her teeth. She would just have to build a fire without the flash heater, using skills she had been taught on Dathomir.

It took an agonizingly long time for her strong arms to produce enough friction twirling one smooth stick of wood against a flat branch. Finally, she managed to coax forth a glowing ember and a tendril of smoke. Working quickly, she touched a dried leaf to it and blew. A tiny golden flame licked its way up the leaf. With mounting excitement she added another and then another, and then a few twigs.

A gust of wind threatened to extinguish the struggling flame, so she encircled her fire with a tiny earthen berm to protect it. She added more tinder, and soon the snapping blaze was large enough to warm her and cast a comforting circle of light.

Tenel Ka soon realized that the restless sounds of scratching and stirring she had heard earlier had grown louder—much louder.

Suddenly, a shrieking reptilian form plummeted from the ceiling, its leathery wings outstretched. Twin serpentine heads snapped and a scorpion tail lashed, razor-sharp claws outstretched. Tenel Ka raised an arm to protect her face as the thing drove directly at her. Talons raked her arm as she pushed herself backward toward the cave wall. Sharp fangs opened a gash in her bare leg, and she kicked fiercely, striking one of the creature's two heads with her scaled boot. In the flickering light from the tiny fire, Tenel Ka watched in horror as an entire flock of the hideous creatures—each with a wingspan wider than she was tall—dropped from the shadowy recesses of the cave and swarmed toward her.

She struggled for purchase on the sandy cave floor and pushed her feet against the stone wall. Tenel Ka propelled herself toward the mouth of the cave on her hands and knees.

She kicked the embers of her fire at the flapping beasts as she scrambled past, hardly noticing the bits of charred wood and leaf that singed her own legs. One of the reptilian creatures shrieked in pain.

Tenel Ka smiled with grim satisfaction and launched herself through the cave opening, back out into the pitch blackness of the jungle night.

The monsters followed.

# 14

AT GUNPOINT, THE TIE pilot led his captives back to the clearing with the small, crude shelter where he had lived for some time.

"So this is why you came running," Jaina said to her brother. "You found where he lives." Jacen nodded.

"Silence!" the Imperial soldier said in a brusque voice.

Jaina, her throat tight and dry, swallowed hard and looked around at the small, cleared site in the gathering evening shadows. Beside them a shallow stream trickled past. She couldn't imagine how the TIE pilot had survived all alone, without any human contact, for so many years.

The climate of Yavin 4 was warm and hospitable, placing few demands on the home the TIE pilot had created for himself. He had carved out a large shelter from the bole of a half-burned Massassi tree, in front of which he had lashed a lean-to of split branches. Altogether, it provided him with a simple but comfortable room, like a living cave. Jaina tried to imagine how long it had taken the Imperial, scraping with a sharp implement—possibly a piece of wreckage from his crashed ship—to widen the area under the gnarled overhang.

The TIE pilot had rigged a system of plumbing made from hollow reeds joined together, drawing water from the nearby stream into catch basins inside his hut. He had made rough utensils from wood, forest gourds, and petrified fungus slabs. The man had maintained a lonely existence, unchallenged, simply surviving and waiting for further orders, hoping someone would come to retrieve him—but no one ever had.

The Imperial soldier stopped outside the hut. "On the ground," he said. "Both of you. Hands above your heads."

Jaina looked at Jacen as they lay belly-down on the ground of the clearing. She could think of no way to escape. The TIE pilot went to the thick foliage and rummaged among the branches with his good hand. He wrapped his fingers around some thin, purplish vines that dangled from dazzlingly bright Nebula orchids in the branches above his head. With a jerk he snapped the strands free.

The vine tendrils flopped and writhed in his grip as if they were alive and trying to squirm away. The TIE pilot rapidly used them to lash Jaina's wrists together, then Jacen's. As the deep violet sap leaked from the broken ends of the vines, the plant's thrashing slowed, and the flexible, rubbery vines contracted, tightening into knots that were impossible to break.

Jacen and Jaina looked at each other, their liquid-brown eyes meeting as a host of thoughts gleamed unspoken between them. But they said nothing, afraid to anger their captor.

Marching clumsily through the humid jungle had made them hot and sticky, and Jaina was still covered with grime from her repairs on the TIE fighter's engines. Now the cool jungle evening chilled her perspiration and made her shiver. Her hands tingled and throbbed, as the tight vines cutting into her wrists made her even more miserable.

In the hour or so since their capture, neither of the twins had heard any further sign of Lowie or Tenel Ka. Jaina was afraid that something had happened to them, that her two friends were even now stranded and lost somewhere in the jungle. But then she realized that her own situation was probably a lot more dangerous than theirs.

Without a word, the TIE pilot nudged them

to their feet, then over to the large lava-rock boulders near the fire pit he used outside his shelter. They squatted there together. The stone chairs had been polished smooth, their sharp edges chipped away slowly and patiently over the course of years by the lost Imperial.

The last coppery rays of light from the huge orange planet Yavin disappeared, as the rapidly rotating moon covered the jungle with night. Through the densely laced treetops, thick shadows gathered, making the forest floor darker than the deepest night on Jacen and Jaina's glittering home planet of Coruscant.

The Imperial pilot walked over to the splintered chunks of dry, moss-covered wood he had painstakingly gathered, one-armed, and stacked near his shelter. He carried them back and dropped one branch at a time into the fire pit, stacking the wood in formation to make a small campfire.

The pilot withdrew a battered igniter from a storage bin inside his shelter and pointed it at the campfire. Its charge had been nearly depleted, and the silvery nozzle showered only a few hot sparks onto the kindling; but he seemed accustomed to such difficulties. He toiled in silence, never cursing, never complaining, simply focused on the task of

getting the campfire lit. And when he succeeded, he showed no satisfaction, no joy.

With the fire finally blazing, the TIE pilot
ducked back inside his hut, rummaged in a
vine-woven basket, and returned with a large
spherical fruit. The fruit was encased in an
ugly, warty brown rind. Jaina did not recognize it. It was nothing they ate at the Jedi
academy.

Holding it in his injured, gauntleted hand,
the pilot used a sharpened stone to split open
the rind, then peeled the fruit with his fingers. The flesh inside was pale yellowish-
green, speckled with scarlet. He broke the
fruit into sections, shuffled over to the two
captives, and pushed one of the fruit sections
in Jaina's face. "Eat."

She clamped her lips together for a moment, afraid that the Imperial soldier might
be trying to poison her. Then she realized
that the TIE pilot could have killed either of
them at any time—and that she was extremely hungry and thirsty.

Her hands still bound by the drying vine,
she leaned forward and opened her mouth to
bite into the bright fruit. The explosion of
tart citrus-tasting juice proved surprisingly
invigorating and delicious. She chewed
slowly, savoring the taste, and swallowed.

Jacen also ate his. They nodded their

thanks to the TIE pilot, who fixed them with a stony gaze.

Sensing an opening, Jacen asked, "What are you going to do with us, sir?" He tried to rub his chin against his shoulder to wipe off the juice dribbling from his lips.

The TIE pilot stared unnervingly at him for several moments before he turned his face toward the bushes. "Not yet determined."

Jaina's chest muscles constricted. All of this had been an accident, a mistake. From the thick bushes, the TIE pilot had probably watched them tinker with his ruined ship for days. But Jacen's accidental discovery of his primitive shelter had forced him to react.

What could the Imperial soldier do with them? He didn't seem to have many options.

"What's your name?" Jaina asked.

The TIE pilot snapped upright and looked down at the black leather glove covering his twisted arm. He turned slowly toward her, like a droid with worn-out servomotors. "CE3K-1977." He rattled off the numbers as if he had memorized them. Service rank and operating number only.

"Not your number," Jaina persisted. "Your name. I'm Jaina. This is my brother Jacen."

"CE3K-1977," the TIE pilot said again, without emotion.

"Your *name*?" Jaina asked a third time.

Finally her question seemed to perplex

him. He looked at the ground, looked at his tattered uniform. His mouth opened and closed several times, but no sound came out, until finally he said in a croaking voice, "Qorl . . . Qorl. My name was Qorl."

"We're staying at the academy in the old temples," Jacen said, wearing a small grin— the kind that always disarmed their mother when she was angry at him. But it didn't seem to be working with the TIE pilot.

"Rebel base," Qorl said.

"No, it's a school now," Jaina said. "Everyone's there to learn. It's not a base any longer. It hasn't been a base for . . . twenty years or so."

"It is a Rebel base," Qorl insisted with such finality that Jaina decided not to pursue the subject any further.

"How did you get here?" she asked, leaning closer on the smooth rock. The campfire crackled between them. "How long have you lived in the jungle?" The tight vines constricting her circulation made her hands numb. She flexed her fingers as she bent toward the fire. The smoke smelled rich and sweet from the fresh jungle wood.

The TIE pilot blinked his pale eyes and stared into the crackling flames. He looked as if he had been transported back in time and was watching a newsloop of his own buried memories.

"Death Star," Qorl said. "I was on the Death Star. We came here to destroy the Rebel base after Grand Moff Tarkin blew up Alderaan. This was our next target."

Jaina felt a pang as she remembered her mother talking of the lovely grass-covered planet Alderaan, the peaceful windsongs and tall towers rising above the plains. Princess Leia's home had been the heart of galactic culture and civilization—until it was wiped out in a single blow by the incredible cruelty of the Empire.

"We must obliterate the Rebels at all costs," Qorl continued. "Rebels cause damage to the Empire."

He recited a litany of what seemed to be memorized phrases, thoughts that had been brainwashed into him. "The Emperor's New Order will save the galaxy. The Rebels want to destroy that dream, and so we must eradicate the Rebels. They are a cancer to peace and stability."

"You were on the Death Star," Jacen prompted. "That was over twenty years ago. What happened?"

Qorl continued to stare deeply into the fire. His scratchy voice was barely more than a whisper. "The Rebels knew we were coming. They fought. They sent their defenses against the battle station. All TIE squadrons were launched.

"I flew with my squadron. All my companions were destroyed by X-wing defensive fire. I was damaged in the cross fire . . . one solar panel out of commission. I spun away from the Death Star, out of control.

"I needed to get back to effect repairs. All comm channels were jammed, filled with dozens of requests for assistance. My orbit was decaying, and I spun toward the fourth moon of Yavin. I kept trying to hail someone on the comm channels. When I finally got through, I was told I would have to wait for rescue. They instructed me to make a good landing if I could—and to wait."

"So you crashed," Jaina said.

"The jungle cushioned my fall. I was thrown out of my craft into the dense brush . . . when one of the solar panels caught and lodged in the trees above. I limped over to my TIE fighter. Stayed as close as I dared, afraid that it might explode. My arm—" He held up his left arm in the black leather gauntlet. "Badly injured, ligaments torn, bones broken.

"I looked up into the sky just in time to see the Death Star blow up. It was like another sun in the sky. Flaming chunks of debris fell through the air. It must have started dozens of forest fires. For weeks, meteor showers were like fireworks as the wreckage rained down onto the moon.

"And I stayed here."

The firelight bathed Qorl's face with a dancing, yellowish glow. The jungle sounds burred in a hypnotic hum all around them. The TIE pilot gave no sign that he realized his two captives were listening. Only his lips moved as he continued his tale.

"I have waited here, and waited, as ordered. No one has come to rescue me."

"But," Jaina said, "all those years! This place has been abandoned for quite some time, but people have been at the Jedi academy for eleven years now. Why haven't you turned yourself in? Don't you realize what's happened in the galaxy since you crashed?"

"Surrender is betrayal!" Qorl snapped, glaring at her as anger flickered across his weathered face.

"But we're not lying," Jacen said. "The war is over. There *is* no more Empire." He took a deep breath and then plunged ahead. "Darth Vader is dead. The Emperor is dead. The New Republic now rules. Only a few remnants of old Imperial holdouts are still buried in the Core Systems at the center of the galaxy."

"I don't believe you," Qorl said flatly.

"If you take us back to the Jedi academy we can prove it. We can show you everything," Jaina said. "Wouldn't you like to go home?

Wouldn't you like to be free of this place? We could get your arm treated."

Qorl held up his glove and stared at it. "I used my medi-kit," he said. "I tended it as best I could. It is good enough, although there was much pain . . . for a long time."

"But we've got Jedi healers!" Jaina said. "We've got medical droids. You could be happy again. Why stay here? There's nothing to betray: there is no more Empire."

"Be quiet," Qorl said. "The Empire will always rule. The Emperor is invincible."

"The Emperor is dead," Jacen said.

"The Empire itself can never die," Qorl insisted.

"But if you won't let us take you back to get help, then what do you *want*?" Jaina asked.

Jacen nodded, chiming in. "What are you trying to accomplish?"

"What can we do for you, Qorl?"

The TIE pilot turned away from the campfire to stare at them. His haggard, weatherbeaten face held new power and obsession, springing from deep within his mind.

"You will finish repairs to my ship," he said. "And then I shall fly away from this prison moon. I'll return to the Empire as a glorious hero of war. Surrender is betrayal—and I *never* surrendered."

"And what if we won't help you?" Jacen said with all the bravado he could manage.

Jaina instantly wanted to kick him for provoking the TIE pilot.

Qorl looked at the young boy, his face coldly expressionless again. "Then you are expendable," he said.

# 15

IT TOOK EM TEEDEE several moments to recalibrate his sensors after he dropped from Lowbacca's fiber-belt. He had fallen, bouncing, crashing, and bonking through the canopy until he finally came to rest on a dense mat of leafy vines that tied together the lower branches.

"Master Lowbacca, come back!" he said, amplifying his voice circuits to their maximum volume levels. "Don't leave me! Oh, dear. I *knew* that was a bad idea."

He adjusted his optical sensors so he could see better in the dim light of the lower levels. He was surrounded by thickets that were nearly inaccessible to anyone as large as even a young Wookiee.

"Help! Help me!" Em Teedee shouted again. He decided it would be most effective to continue shouting every forty-five seconds, because he calculated that was the minimum amount of time necessary for anyone nearby to come within earshot.

Unable to move and scout out his location, Em Teedee's best guess was that he was still twenty meters above the ground. He hoped that no slight jarring of the branches would cause him to break free and tumble down again. If he fell that far to the ground, he might strike one of the rough lava outcroppings and split open his outer casing. With his circuits spilled across the jungle floor, no one would ever be able to put him back together again in the proper fashion. His circuits buzzed at the thought.

Forty-five seconds had passed. He called out again for help, then waited. He shouted repeatedly for the next hour and eleven minutes, hoping desperately to attract some sort of attention, someone to come rescue him.

But when he finally did attract a curious investigator, Em Teedee wished he had kept his vocal circuits switched off.

A large pack of chattering woolamanders scurried through the lower canopy, stirring up leaves and cracking twigs in their hectic passage. The arboreal creatures were loud and agile, able to clamber from thin branches to thick ones and back again without losing their balance. They seemed to be engaged in a contest to see who could yowl and chatter the loudest in the jungle silence as twilight deepened.

Somehow, over all the ruckus, they managed to hear Em Teedee's cries for help.

Em Teedee knew from his limited database of Yavin 4 that woolamanders were curious, social creatures. Now that they had heard him, they began to search. In only moments, with their sharp, slit-eyed vision, they had spotted the translator droid's shiny outer casing in the jungle shadows. The pack of colorful, hairy creatures swarmed toward him.

"Oh, no," Em Teedee cried. "Not you. Please—I was hoping for someone *else* to rescue me."

The woolamanders came closer, rattling branches, rustling leaves. Their bright purple fur bristled with suspicion and delight.

"Go away! Shoo!" Em Teedee said.

The woolamanders let out a loud, shrieking celebration of their discovery. A large male snatched Em Teedee from his resting place in the vines.

"Put me down," Em Teedee said. "I *insist* that you let go of me at once."

The large male tossed Em Teedee to his mate, who caught the translator droid and turned him over and around, poking at the shiny circles. She dug her grimy finger into the gold circle of his optical sensors.

"That's my eye—get your finger away from it! Now I'm upside down. Straighten me out . . . put me down!"

The female shook and rattled him to see if he would make other noises. When she went to a thick branch and made ready to smash him down on it, as she would crack open a large fruit, Em Teedee set off his automatic alarm sirens, shrieking and whooping at such volume and at such a painful pitch that the female dropped him. He bounced on another leafy branch, then came precariously to rest.

"Help!" Em Teedee wailed.

One of the smaller woolamanders rushed in to snatch him from his resting place. With loud chattering and squeals of delight, the young woolamander dashed along the lower branches, holding his prize high as Em Teedee continued to howl for assistance. The other young woolamanders chased after the youngster, clamoring for the prize.

Em Teedee, in such a panic that he could no longer stand it without overloading his circuits, shut down so he wouldn't have to see what was about to happen to him.

Sometime late in the night he powered back on again to find that he could see nothing: his optical sensors were covered with thick fur.

He detected a gentle motion . . . breathing, snoring. Then the young woolamander stirred in its sleep. It shifted, allowing Em Teedee to discover that the small creature now lay sleeping in the crotch of a tree branch, contentedly hugging his new toy to his fur-covered chest.

Around them, the other family members of the large arboreal group sighed and dozed, resting peacefully. Em Teedee had an impulse to cry out again for help, still hoping that someone might come to rescue him.

All the noisy woolamanders were finally asleep, though, and Em Teedee decided to treasure this moment of peace. He could only hope for something better to happen the next day.

# 16

DAWN CAME FAST and hot, as the distant white sun climbed around the fuzzy ball of Yavin. Jungle creatures awoke and stirred. The air warmed rapidly, thick with humidity that rose from low hollows where mist had collected in the night.

Jacen and Jaina had slept awkwardly, their hands still tied with the resilient purple vines. Jacen fervently wished he had spent more time practicing delicate and precise Force exercises. He didn't have the skill or the accuracy to nudge and untie the thin knotted vines with his mind.

As soon as there was light enough to work, Qorl emerged from his tree shelter and shook the twins awake. He gave them each sips of cool water from a gourd he dipped in the stream, then used a long stone knife to saw off the vines binding their wrists.

Jacen flexed his fingers and shook out his

hands. His nerves tingled and stung with returning circulation.

The Imperial soldier pointed the blaster at them, gesturing for the twins to move. "Back to the TIE fighter," he ordered. "Work."

Jacen and Jaina trudged through the jungle, stumbling through vines and shrubs; the TIE pilot followed directly behind them. They reached the site of the crashed ship, where it lay uncovered and glinting in the early morning light. With a knot forming in his stomach, Jacen saw burned patches from where Qorl had shot his blaster at Tenel Ka and Lowie.

"I know you are nearly finished with repairs," the TIE pilot said. "I have been watching you for days. You will complete them today."

Jaina blinked her brandy-brown eyes and scowled at him. "We can't possibly work that fast, especially with just the two of us. This ship has been crashed for twenty years. We haven't finished cleaning the debris from the sublight intakes. The power converters all need to be rewired."

Jacen watched his sister and knew she was lying.

"Cyberfuses still need to be installed," she continued. "The air-exchange system is clogged; it needs to be—"

Qorl raised the blaster, but did not alter the

emotion in his voice. *"Today,"* he repeated. "You will finish today."

"Oh, blaster bolts! I think he means it, Jaina," Jacen muttered. "Show me what I can do to help."

Jaina sighed. "All right. Collect the box of tools you tripped over yesterday. Get the hydrospanner. I'll use my multitool to finish some calibrations here in the engines."

Qorl sat down on a lumpy, lichen-encrusted boulder, using his good hand to brush crawling insects from his legs. The Imperial soldier waited like a droid sentinel, unmoving, watching them work. Jacen tried to ignore him—and the blaster.

Gnats and biting insects swarmed around Jacen's face, attracted by the sweat in his tangled hair. He passed tools to his sister, trying to find the components and equipment Jaina needed as she crawled and rummaged in the TIE fighter's engine compartment.

He could sense Jaina's growing anger and frustration. She couldn't think of a plan. Yes, Jacen supposed, they could simply sabotage the ship repairs—but Qorl would realize what they'd done almost immediately, and he would get even with them. They couldn't risk that.

Now Jacen wished that his sister, in all her excitement, hadn't installed the new hyperdrive unit their dad had given her. He wished that they all hadn't worked so hard, made so much progress. Now it was almost too late.

Jacen brushed a hand across his forehead, blinking sweat away. His stomach growled. He turned to the TIE pilot, sitting nearby on the rock, still pointing the blaster barrel directly at him. The threat was getting tiresome.

"Qorl," he said, intentionally using their captor's real name. "Could we have some water and more fruit? We're hungry. We'll work better if we're not hungry."

Qorl nodded slightly and began to stand up. But then he froze, hesitated, and settled back into his rigid position. "Food and water when you are finished with repairs."

"What? " Jacen said in dismay. "But that could take all day."

"Then you will be hungry and thirsty," Qorl said. The TIE pilot looked somewhat anxious, impatient. "You are stalling. Proceed."

Jacen realized that Qorl might be worried that either Tenel Ka or Lowie had managed to get back to the Jedi academy and summoned help. They were a long distance from the Great Temple, across a treacherous jungle . . . but there was always a chance.

Jaina finished adjusting a cooling system regulator. She twisted a knob; a cold, bright blast of supercooled steam screeched up, making feathers of frost on the exposed metal surface. She stepped back and rubbed a grimy hand across her cheek, leaving a dark stain beneath her liquid-brown eyes.

"Qorl?" she said. "Who are you going to see when you get back?"

"I will report for duty," he said.

"Are you going home? Do you have a family?"

"The Empire is my family." His answer was rapid, automatic.

"But do you have a family that *loves you*?" Jaina asked.

Qorl hesitated for the briefest moment, then gestured threateningly with the blaster. "Get back to work."

Jaina sighed and motioned for her brother to help her. "Come on, Jacen. Take those last packages of surface metal sealant," she said. "We need to reinforce the melt spots on the outer hull." She pointed to three stained and vaporized bull's-eye spots on the TIE fighter's outer plating—damage Qorl himself had caused the day before by firing his blaster at the twins.

With a cushioned hammer, Jaina pounded the bent plates back into position. Jacen dug into the toolbox until he found a packet of animated metal sealant. The special paste would crawl across the damaged area, smooth itself, and then seal down with a bond even stronger than the original hull alloy. Jacen applied one packet of the patch material and listened to it hiss and steam as it coated the burn spot. Jaina fixed the second spot.

The third melted area lay high on the cargo compartment, close to the open transparisteel canopy that protected the cockpit. Jacen took the last pack and crawled atop the small craft. He popped the seal, applied the patch, and waited for the animated sealant to do its work.

As he watched the gooey substance finish its repairs, Jacen heard small creatures stirring around him. He sensed something nearby and, looking down into the cargo space, saw a glimmer of movement, almost transparent, barely noticeable. Jacen's heart leaped. He leaned down, reaching deep into the TIE fighter, and grabbed for it. Hope began to fill him.

"Boy, get out of there!" Qorl yelled. "Come back where I can see you."

Panting, his heart pounding, Jacen pulled himself free. He backed away from the cockpit and jumped to the ground, keeping his hands clearly in sight.

Jaina bent over and whispered to him with concern in her eyes. "What are you doing? What did you find in there?"

Jacen grinned at her, then recovered his

expression before Qorl could notice it. "Something that might save us all."

"No more talking," Qorl snapped. "Hurry."

"We're doing the best we can," Jaina replied.

"Not good enough," the pilot said. "Do you need encouragement? If you cannot complete repairs faster, I will shoot your brother. Then you will complete the repairs by yourself."

Both Jacen and Jaina looked at the TIE pilot in shock. "Qorl, you wouldn't do that," Jaina said.

"I received my training from the Empire," Qorl answered. "I will do what is necessary."

Jacen swallowed—he knew the TIE pilot was telling the truth. "Yeah, I'll bet you would," he said.

With a sigh and an expression of disgust, Jaina stood up and tossed the hydrospanner onto a pile of tools on the jungle floor. She brushed her hands down her thighs, wiping grime on the legs of her jumpsuit.

"Never mind," she said. "It's finished. We've done everything we can. The TIE fighter is ready to fly again."

# 17

INSIDE THE TORCHLIT temples of the Jedi academy, Lowbacca bellowed in confusion and alarm. He waved his lanky, hairy arms to emphasize the urgency of the situation. He didn't know how to make them understand him; he only knew he had to warn them of the TIE fighter, had to get help for Jacen and Jaina and Tenel Ka.

Tionne and the other Jedi candidates around her grew agitated. None of them could speak the Wookiee language. "Lowbacca, we can't understand you," she said. "Where is your translator droid?"

Lowie patted his hip again and made a distressed sound. He'd have never imagined he'd be so upset not to have the jabbering droid at his side.

"Where are Jacen, Jaina, and Tenel Ka?" Tionne asked. "Are they all right?"

Lowbacca bellowed again and gestured out into the jungle, trying to explain everything.

"Was there an accident? Are they hurt?" Tionne asked. Her mother-of-pearl eyes were wide and her silver hair flowed about her as if it were alive. With her long, delicate hands, she clutched Lowie's furred arm.

Her voice had been so calm and silky when she sang Jedi ballads to the gathered students in the grand audience chamber. Now her words had a hard, crystalline edge, the forcefulness of a true Jedi Knight.

Lowbacca tried to think of how to explain, but his growing frustration made it more and more difficult. He had no words they could understand. Yes, he could gesture back toward the jungle—but how to describe a crashed TIE fighter? A surviving Imperial pilot? The twins taken hostage?

The young Jedi Knights had kept their little project completely secret while they were making repairs to the crashed ship. Jaina had wanted the revamped craft to be a surprise she could show off to the other trainees. But now having kept it a secret was working against them. No one could guess what he was talking about; no one knew about the crash site.

He didn't know what had happened to Tenel Ka, either. Had she been killed, or had she somehow escaped? Was she even now lost in the jungles by herself, being stalked by predators? He moaned in dismay.

Unable to restrain himself, Lowie rattled off the whole story in loud Wookiee grunts and roars. Everyone around him grew agitated, unable to decipher a word he was saying. Finally, his frustration got the best of him: Lowie pounded his fists on one of the stone walls and pushed past Tionne and the other Jedi candidates into the cool shadows of the Great Temple.

"Where are you going, Lowbacca?" Tionne called, but he didn't answer her.

Though Lowie was still tired, the others could not catch up with him. With only the slightest limp, his long, muscular legs carried him down the winding corridors of the ancient stone ruin. Breathless, he reached the room that had been the old command center when the temple served as a Rebel base. Luke Skywalker maintained it to keep contact with the rest of the New Republic.

He knew his uncle Chewbacca was still in the Yavin system, near the orange gas giant where Lando Calrissian had set up his orbiting mining facility for Corusca gems. If only Lowie could get in touch with the *Millennium Falcon*, speak to his uncle, he could explain everything directly. Chewbacca—along with Jacen and Jaina's father, Han Solo—would know just what to do.

With a loud sigh of relief, Lowie sank into a chair in front of a console. The station was filled with the only things in the Jedi academy that seemed familiar to him at this moment: the computers and electronic equipment. He knew exactly how to communicate with them.

Lowbacca worked the controls with speed and determination, tapping his clawed fingers over the appropriate buttons. He had already established an open channel to the *Falcon* by the time Tionne and the others caught up with him in the Communications Center.

Tionne immediately realized what he was doing, and she nodded. "Good idea, Lowbacca!" She waited beside the young Wookiee as a sleepy-sounding Han Solo answered the call.

"Yeah, this is Solo. Who's calling? Luke? Is this the Jedi academy?" Lowbacca bleated into the microphone pickup, hoping the human pilot would understand him.

Tionne leaned over next to Lowbacca before he could continue and spoke into the voice pickup. "Something has happened here, General Solo. The twins and Tenel Ka have disappeared, and Lowbacca is trying to tell us what happened. But he can't make us understand him. He's lost his translator droid."

With a roar of surprise, Chewbacca came on the line. Excited, Lowie once again ex-

plained everything as fast as he could in the
Wookiee language. Chewbacca roared back
in outrage, and Han broke in.

"Quiet, old buddy. I heard most of that, but
a few of the details were sketchy. Something
about a crashed TIE fighter and an Imperial
soldier taking them hostage?"

Both Wookiees made loud sounds of agreement.

"Okay, sit tight. We're on our way!" Han
said. "We can undock from Lando's station in
just a few seconds. We were ready to get out
of here anyway. The *Falcon*'ll be there in
about two hours—middle of the local morning, I think. Just hold on and get ready to
help me fight for the kids!"

Lowie and Chewbacca both bellowed in
agreement. Tionne looked at the young
Wookiee in amazement. "A TIE fighter! Imperials here? Quick, we must get everyone
ready in case they attack."

With a searing white flicker from its aft
sublight engines, the *Millennium Falcon*
cruised through the deep blue atmosphere
toward the ancient Massassi structures.
Lowie stood in the open landing area in front
of the Great Temple, anxious to see his uncle.
He waved his shaggy arms for the ship as it
approached.

The bright light of morning grew warmer

with each passing minute. The two hours it had taken for the *Millennium Falcon* to leave the Yavin gas giant and approach the jungle moon had seemed the longest of Lowie's life.

Now he stepped back into the shade of the temple as the *Falcon* settled to the ground with hissing bursts of its repulsorlift engines. The landing pads settled and stabilized, and then the boarding ramp came down like an opening mouth.

Chewbacca bounded down the ramp, ducking his hairy head to keep from bumping the low ceiling, and headed toward the temple. Lowie ran to meet him halfway, limping slightly. Han Solo charged out and joined them, his blaster already drawn.

"Ready to rescue the kids? Let's go!" Han said. Tionne and several of the other Jedi candidates hurried out. Han looked around. "Where's Luke? Isn't he back yet?"

"Master Skywalker isn't here," Tionne said. "We have to defend *ourselves*."

"We'll take care of it," Han said. "Lando gave us some extra weapons, and all our laser cannon banks are charged. Lowie, can you show us where they're being held?"

Lowbacca nodded his shaggy head.

"If there are any more Imperial TIE fighters around," Han said, "the most important thing you can do is guard the Jedi academy, Tionne. This would be their obvious target.

The Empire doesn't particularly like the New Republic getting another batch of Jedi Knights."

"We'll be here to defend the academy, General Solo," Tionne said. "You find the children."

"All right, Lowie," Han said. "Let's go—no time to waste."

# 18

THE ROAR OF twin ion engines shattered the deep stillness of the jungle morning as the TIE fighter returned to life. Birds squawked in terror and fled into the high branches. Dust and dry, crumbling leaves scattered in clouds around the Imperial ship.

Encased in the cockpit, Qorl throttled up the power, slowly, gently, as if feeling it grow at his fingertips. Foul brownish exhaust spat out of the clogged vent ports in the rear of the single-fighter craft. The Imperial ship growled, ready for action again after its long retirement.

The TIE pilot emerged from the cockpit, his battered black helmet in hand, the respirator hoses dangling and disconnected from his empty emergency-oxygen supply. Although the glossy blast goggles had been scratched and worn down during the years of his exile, he carried the helmet proudly, like a trophy.

Qorl was ready to report back to duty.

"Propulsion systems check out," he said. "With the addition of the functional hyperdrive motor you installed, I am now able to cross the galaxy and find the remnants of my Empire. This short-range fighter could not otherwise have taken me there."

"Good work, Jaina," Jacen grumbled. She elbowed him in the ribs, and he fell silent.

"What are you going to do with us, Qorl?" Jaina asked the pilot. "Why go away from here? If you'd just come back with us to the Jedi academy, everything would be all right—the war is over."

"Surrender is betrayal!" Qorl shouted, with a surge of emotion stronger than Jacen had seen in him before. The pilot's hand shook as he pointed the ever-present blaster at them. "Your usefulness to me is at an end," he said, his voice a low threat.

Jacen's stomach clenched with sudden dread. Jaina had hoped to make the TIE fighter her own vehicle so she could joyride just like Lowie did in his revamped T-23. But the small fighter could carry only one person: the pilot. Qorl could never take them along as prisoners, even if he wanted to. Would the pilot remove his last obstacles—the only witnesses to his exile—with clean Imperial efficiency? Would he just shoot them both and then fly off in search of his home?

Jacen desperately tried to send calming thoughts to soothe Qorl, as he so frequently did with his crystal snakes. But it was no use: his mind encountered the rigid wall of brainwashing that had locked Qorl's thoughts into unchangeable patterns.

The TIE pilot looked away, and his temper seemed to lessen. Jacen couldn't tell if that was a result of his Jedi powers or if the Imperial soldier had simply been distracted.

"So what *are* you going to do with us?" Jacen asked.

Qorl glanced back at the twins, his face haggard. He looked very old and drained. "You have helped me a great deal. You were the only . . . company I have had for many years. I will leave you here alone in the jungle."

"You're just going to abandon us?" Jaina asked in disbelief. This time, Jacen elbowed *her* in the ribs. He didn't relish the idea of being stranded in the jungle any more than she did, but several less-appealing possibilities had occurred to him.

"You can survive if you are resourceful," Qorl said. "I know, because I did. Perhaps someone will find you eventually. Hope is your best weapon. It may not take twenty years for *you* to get home."

He pondered for a moment, holding his dark helmet in his hands. Behind him, the repaired TIE fighter continued to purr, as if anxious to fly again. "You are lucky to be here, safe," Qorl finally said. "I will rejoin the Empire. But as my last act here on this cursed jungle moon, I am going to destroy the Rebel base."

"No!" Jacen and Jaina both shouted in unison.

"It's just a school now. It's not a military base," Jacen added.

"Please don't do this!" Jaina said. "Don't attack the Jedi academy."

But Qorl gave no sign that he heard them. He carefully placed the battered old helmet on his shaggy head and tightened down the blast shield.

"Wait!" Jaina cried, her eyes pleading. "They have no weapons in the temples!" She reached out with her mind, trying to touch the pilot, but he aimed his blaster at her and backed away.

Qorl climbed into the cockpit of the TIE fighter, eased himself into the ancient, torn seat in front of the controls, and sealed himself in. The twins rushed forward, pounding on the hull with their fists.

The roar of the engines increased and the repulsorlifts sent out a blast that knocked leaves, pebbles, and jungle debris in all directions.

The TIE fighter hummed, shifted from its overgrown resting place, and began to rise.

Jaina tried one last time to grab the hull plates, but her fingers slid along the smooth metal. Jacen pulled her back as the TIE's engine power increased. The exhaust shrieked through the fighter's cooling systems.

The twins staggered back under the protection of one of the overarching Massassi trees, alone and defenseless in the thick jungles.

Qorl's TIE fighter, which had lain hidden and crippled on the surface of Yavin 4 for more than twenty years, finally rose into the air. Its twin ion engines made the characteristic moaning sound that had struck fear into the hearts of so many Rebel fighters.

With surprisingly skillful maneuvering and a burst of speed, Qorl's fighter climbed up through the forest canopy and soared away toward the Jedi academy.

# 19

IN THE DARKNESS of the jungle night, Tenel Ka plunged through tangled vines and dense, thorny thickets, hoping that the flying reptiles would not be able to follow. She panted from the exertion; breath burned in her lungs, but she did not cry out.

She could still hear the flap of the reptiles' wide, leathery wings close behind her as they swooped in for the kill with their razor talons. The raucous cries of their hideous twin heads chilled her blood. She remembered hearing that such a beast had almost killed Master Skywalker many years ago. How did the monsters manage to maneuver in the crowded jungle? she wondered. Why couldn't she lose them?

The bushes beside her hissed and rattled, and a stinger tail narrowly missed her arm. One of the winged monsters was directly above her, then. What could she do?

She pushed through a narrower space between two trees and heard a *thump* above her as the flying creature got stuck in the opening between the trees. *Good*, she thought. The rest would have to go around. That would buy her some time.

Tenel Ka pelted across a clearing toward the shadow of what she hoped was another patch of underbrush, but she had misjudged the speed with which the reptilian creatures could nagivate the jungle obstacles. She could feel the menacing wind from their wings as one of them swooped down directly in her path.

She sensed, rather than saw, the outstretched claws, and tried to turn aside, but slipped on rotting vegetation and fell hard against a fungus-covered log. She sensed a second pair of claws rip through the air where her stomach had been only moments before. She shuddered as twin heads cried out in rage and frustration above her, tearing at thick, tangled twigs in the brush.

Why couldn't she remember her Jedi calming techniques when she needed them? Why hadn't she practiced harder? She closed her eyes, *sensed*, and rolled to one side as the flying monster drove down for another attack.

The sound of dozens of wings overhead prodded her back into motion. She rolled onto her bare hands and knees, scrambled through some low thornbushes, pushed herself to her feet, and kept running.

*Sense*, she told herself. *Use the Force.*

Suddenly, she changed direction, as if by reflex. She didn't quite know why she had, for she couldn't see where she was going in the thick night, but she knew she was right. Over and over, she dodged grasping talons and the thrust of stinging tails, until she came to a thick stand of Massassi trees. At her noisy approach, a chorus of squawks and scolding chitters erupted from the trees ahead.

Woolamanders—an entire pack, from the sound of them. She had probably disturbed their communal sleep. Perhaps they would be sufficient distraction.

Tenel Ka crouched low and dove into the shelter of the close-growing trees. Surprisingly, not one of the winged monsters followed. Instead, she heard their cries as they circled above and, deprived of their initial prey, hunted the woolamanders instead. The flying creatures screamed their blood lust, and the voices of the terrified woolamanders became fierce and defiant as the battle raged in the branches far overhead.

Sweat, twigs, leaves, and dirt clung to Tenel Ka's red-gold hair. She shook her head to clear it. She was almost certain that through the racket, she had somehow heard a faint, familiar voice.

"Oh please, *do* be careful. My circuitry is extremely complex and should not under any circumstances be—" The voice cut off a moment later with a tiny wail. Then there was a *thud* as something hard landed beside Tenel Ka's foot.

"Em Teedee, is that you?" she said. She groped around on the ground and picked up the rounded metallic form.

"Oh, Mistress Tenel Ka, it *is* you!" the little droid cried. "I shall be eternally grateful to you for this rescue. Why, you have no idea the ordeal I've been through," he moaned. "The poking, the prodding, the shaking, the tossing. And such a dreadful—"

"My night has been no more enjoyable than yours," Tenel Ka interrupted drily.

"Listen!" Em Teedee said. "Oh, thank goodness! Those dreadful creatures are leaving."

Tenel Ka didn't know whether Em Teedee was referring to the woolamanders or the giant flying reptiles, but she realized that the sounds of the overhead battle were moving farther and farther away through the canopy.

"We must make our escape immediately, Mistress Tenel Ka."

"We can't. We'll have to wait until morning. Can you keep a watch out tonight while I sleep?"

"I'd be delighted to keep a watch for you, Mistress, but *must* we spend the night here?"

"Yes, we must," Tenel Ka snapped, defensive now that the worst danger was over. "I need to wait until daylight so I can climb a tree and find out where we are."

"Oh," said Em Teedee. "But whyever should you want to do something like that?"

Tenel Ka growled, "Because we're lost in the jungle. This is a fact."

"Oh, dear—is *that* all that's bothering you?" Em Teedee said. "Why didn't you say so? After all, I am fluent in six forms of communication *and* I am equipped with all manner of sensors: photo-optical, olfactory, directional, auditory—"

"Directional?" Tenel Ka broke in. "You mean you *know* where we are?"

"Oh, most assuredly, Mistress Tenel Ka. Didn't I just say so?"

She groaned and shook her head. "All right, Em Teedee, let's go. Lead on."

Tenel Ka's spirits were brighter than the twin beams that shone from Em Teedee's eyes and lit her way along the forest floor. As annoying as the little droid could be, she was glad of his company. Em Teedee seemed genuinely interested in hearing all that had happened to her since the TIE fighter pilot had tried to capture them that afternoon. In turn, she found herself enjoying his descriptions of the T-23 crash and his adventures with the woolamanders. She wondered what had happened to Lowbacca, and to the twins.

They stopped only a few times, so that she could drink or check the dressing on her minor wounds. Using rudimentary first-aid supplies she kept in her belt, she had bound up the claw scratches on her arm and the gash on her leg. The wounds throbbed and burned, but did not slow her down. She jogged much of the way, and kept to a fast-paced march even when she needed to rest.

The distant white sun of the Yavin system was bright in the morning sky when Tenel Ka and Em Teedee finally broke through the last stand of trees into the cleared landing area. The sun-warmed stone of the Great Temple glowed like a welcome beacon in the distance.

"Oh, we made it!" Em Teedee said joyfully. Tenel Ka looked around and saw in the center of the clearing a ship that she recognized well: the *Millennium Falcon*.

Running toward the modified light freighter at full speed were two Wookiees, one large and one smaller, and Jacen and Jaina's father, Han Solo. She guessed immediately what mission they were on and changed her course toward the *Falcon*, waving and shouting as she ran.

Overhead, she heard the bone-chilling howl of a fast-approaching TIE fighter. She put on another burst of speed toward the ship.

But Solo and the Wookiees did not see her. In their hurry to rescue Jacen and Jaina, the three scrambled up the ramp of the *Falcon*. They must have kept the engines idling to keep them warm, she figured, for she could hear their whine.

Tenel Ka wanted to help rescue the twins; she couldn't let them down again. "Call them, Em Teedee," she said, pouring on a last burst of speed, though her legs already trembled with exhaustion.

Em Teedee mused, "Am I to take it that you wish to communicate with them?"

"This is a fact."

"Certainly, Mistress. I would be delighted, but what shall—"

"Just *do* it!" She gritted her teeth and sprinted as fast as she could.

Suddenly Em Teedee's voice boomed at top volume through the clearing. "Attention, *Millennium Falcon*. Please delay departure momentarily to take on two additional passengers."

Tenel Ka didn't even mind the ringing in her ears when she saw the ramp of the *Millennium Falcon* lower. At full tilt, she ran up the ramp.

"Okay," she gasped, collapsing to the floor in the crew compartment. "Let's go!"

Han Solo and the two Wookiees looked at her in amazement for an instant, but no one needed any further urging. Even as she spoke, the hatches sealed, and with a surge of defiance the *Millennium Falcon* took off.

# 20

QORL FLEW HIS single fighter at top speed over the thick jungle canopy. The rushing air of Yavin 4 screamed around the TIE fighter's rounded pilot compartment and the rectangular solar arrays. He remembered his days as a trainee. He had been an excellent pilot—one of the best in his squadron—soaring through mock battles and enforcing the Emperor's unbending will.

Air currents buffeted him, and the pilot reveled in the sensation of flight. He had not forgotten, not even after so many years. The vibrating power that pulsed through the fighter's engines, along with a sense of freedom and liberation after so long an exile, buoyed him.

Qorl watched the knotted green crowns of Massassi trees flowing beneath him in the storm of his ship's passage. With his thickly gloved, badly healed arm, he found it difficult to control the Imperial craft—but he was a fighter pilot. He was a *great* pilot. He had managed to land his ship, despite grievous engine damage, under heavy enemy fire. He had survived undetected in hostile territory for two decades.

Now, flying low over the trees to avoid notice from any possible defenses at the Rebel base, Qorl felt his memories, his ingrained skill, come flooding back to him.

*The Empire is my family. The Rebels wish to destroy the New Order. The Rebels must be eliminated—ELIMINATED!*

His greatest advantage was surprise. This attack would come out of nowhere. The Rebels would be expecting nothing. He would streak in with all weapons blazing. He would level the Rebel base structures, blast them into rubble. He would kill all those who had conspired to blow up the Death Star, who had killed Darth Vader and Grand Moff Tarkin. He, a single soldier, would secure vengeance for the entire Empire.

There! Qorl squinted through the scratched goggles of his blast helmet. Protruding from a clearing in the dense jungle, a towering stone temple rose up—a ziggurat, the squarish pyramid that served as the main structure of the base.

Qorl roared low over the facilities of the old Rebel stronghold. A wide, sluggish river sliced through the jungle near the site of the temples. On the opposite side of the brownish-green current lay other crumbling ruins, but they seemed uninhabited. Then he noticed a large power-generating station next to the towering ziggurat and knew for certain that he had not been wrong: this base was still used as a military installation.

As he brought the TIE fighter in on his first attack run, Qorl saw that the jungle had been cleared to make a large landing area in front of the Great Temple. On the flat field he saw only one ship—disk-shaped, with twin prongs in front.

Qorl didn't immediately recognize the make or model of the lone ship below. It was some kind of light freighter, not a Rebel X-wing or any of the familiar battleships he had learned about during his rigorous combat training.

On the ground, several people ran toward the ship, sprinting away from the stone pyramid. Scrambling to battle stations perhaps? His lip curled in a snarl. He would take care of them.

He flicked the buttons on his control panel, powering up the TIE fighter's weapons systems. Before he could align the victims in his targeting cross, though, all the small figures below managed to climb aboard the light freighter. Its boarding ramp drew up, preparing for launch.

He dismissed the light freighter as a possible target—for now, at least. It was probable, Qorl realized, that the Rebels kept a large force of more powerful fighters in an underground hangar bay. If so, his first task was to prevent those craft from launching—even if only by damaging the doors enough to keep the ships trapped inside.

He decided his best strategy would be to continue his straight-line course and fire with full-power laser cannons on the main structure of the Great Temple. He would blow the entire building to rubble—perhaps causing it to collapse internally, thus eliminating the Rebels and destroying all their equipment inside.

Then he could swoop around and take care of the single light freighter, even if it managed to get up off the ground. His third target would be the power-generating station.

With the Rebels completely paralyzed by his lightning attack, he would swing back for the last time. He would charge up his laser cannons again and go for the kill, mopping up anything he had missed the first time.

From start to finish, it would take only a few minutes to bring the Rebels to their knees.

Qorl centered the Great Temple in his targeting cross, aiming at the apex of the squared-off pyramid, with its thin banks of skylights and ancient vine-covered sculptures. The TIE fighter zoomed in.

He grasped the firing stick with his good hand. At exactly the right moment he depressed the firing buttons, letting an expression of anticipation light his normally emotionless face.

Nothing.

He squeezed the button again and again—*and nothing happened!* The weapons systems did not respond.

Qorl flicked on the backups as he spun the TIE fighter in the air, barreling down again on his target. Over and over he tried to fire, but the laser cannons were completely dead. His eyes swept the diagnostic panels, but all the readings seemed normal.

With his gloved hand Qorl pounded on the instrumentation panel, as if that would fix anything—and with old Imperial equipment, sometimes it did. But not this time.

He frantically worked with the controls, digging under the panels to restart the weapons systems even as he flew on. He reached down and felt around his seat, searching for anything he could use to jump-start the malfunctioning laser cannons.

Qorl caught the glimmer out of the corner of his eye, reflected against the dark goggles of his helmet. He glanced down and noticed something *moving* . . . sinuous, barely seen, glittering and transparent.

The crystal snake reared up right beside him, its triangular head showing up as a faint rainbow in the glow from the cockpit lights. Qorl, who had seen plenty of the reptilian creatures during his exile on Yavin 4, spotted it immediately and reacted.

He let out a startled cry and tried to brush the snake away. It lunged and bit down as he reached out with his crippled arm to block it. The crystal snake dug its spearlike fangs into the thick leather of Qorl's gauntlet, but was unable to penetrate all the way to his skin.

As he flung his hand back and forth, Qorl could feel the heavy weight of the crystal snake writhing, snapping, though he could see almost nothing at all.

He let the TIE fighter fly itself as he reached with his good hand to grab the long body of the serpent just behind its head. He ripped the fangs free and stuffed the thrashing creature into the cockpit jettison chute. With a cry of disgust he ejected the snake into the air, where it fell toward the treetops of the jungle moon, disappearing instantly in the bright sunlight.

He wrestled for control of his weaponless vessel. The Jedi twins must have done something in their repairs.

He managed to stabilize his erratic flight—

but before he could decide on a new course, bright streaks from an enemy laser cannon sizzled through the air, bolts of energy that ionized the atmosphere around Qorl's TIE fighter.

He yanked at the control stick with his good arm, and his fighter lurched into a starboard spin. The Rebel light freighter had taken to the air and was flying after Qorl like a furious bird of prey. And *its* weapons worked just fine.

Qorl punched in full power to the twin ion engines and decided that his only chance for now was to try to escape.

In the heart of the jungle, next to Qorl's primitive dwelling, Jacen and Jaina sat beside each other, deep in concentration. They reached out with the Force to see what was going on back at the Jedi academy. Their powers were only sufficient to bring them shadowy images, distant echoes of thoughts . . . but it was enough.

"He didn't know I never fixed the weapons systems . . . but then, he never asked. I managed to jury-rig the readouts so they would look normal," Jaina said at last. "He can fly, but his ship is defenseless."

"Yes, and I think the crystal snake must have distracted Qorl somehow," Jacen said.

"I wonder what happened to it." They smiled at each other.

"I suppose our next step," Jacen said, squinting up at the morning light that filtered through the trees, "is to figure out how to get back home."

Jaina pushed a tangle of her usually straight brown hair back from her face and took a deep breath. "Agreed," she said, then clapped her hands and rubbed them together. "So what are we waiting for?"

# 21

"HANG ON!" HAN SOLO yelled.

As the *Millennium Falcon* lifted off from the trampled landing area in front of the ancient temple, Tenel Ka struggled to a seat beside Lowbacca and strapped herself in.

"That TIE fighter's coming in, and it looks mean," Han said as he and his Wookiee copilot frantically set switches and calibrated the weapons targeting systems. "Hope Tionne managed to get all the Jedi trainees to safety."

Their seats tilted back as the *Falcon* angled up into the air, its sublight thrusters roaring behind it. The Imperial TIE fighter broke through the sky overhead like a yowling battering ram.

Han Solo looked grim as he gripped the controls. His jaw was set, his shoulders rigid. At the moment he had no way of knowing whether his children were safe, or if this Imperial enemy had killed them both, just as the pilot had tried to blast Lowbacca and Tenel Ka.

Tenel Ka wished she could give him some reassurance, but she knew nothing herself. Still panting with exhaustion from her long run through the jungle, she adjusted the restraints across the reptilian armor on her chest. At her side Em Teedee's thin, warbly voice spoke up. "I beg your pardon, Mistress Tenel Ka, but I can't see a thing! Your crash webbing has blocked my optical sensors."

When Tenel Ka freed the flat, silvery device from its restraints, Em Teedee let out what sounded like a sigh of relief. "Ah, yes, much better. Now I can see perfectly. Oh, dear!" he said in alarm. "I didn't want you to rescue me from that dreadful jungle just so we could all be blown up chasing that TIE fighter."

Lowbacca grunted and looked over at the small translating droid with obvious surprise and relief.

"This is yours, Lowbacca," Tenel Ka said. "I found it in the jungle." She handed Em Teedee to the young Wookiee, who accepted the little droid gratefully, bleating his thanks.

Han Solo spun the *Falcon* around in a tight arc, its engines rumbling behind them as they pursued the TIE fighter. "He's coming in on an attack run," Han said. "But he's not firing his weapons for some reason."

Through the cockpit windows, Tenel Ka

watched as the TIE fighter she had helped to repair zoomed low over the Great Temple, seemingly bent on destruction—but its laser cannons did not fire.

"I'm going to get his attention, Chewie," Han said. "You open a comm channel. That guy did something to my kids—and I want to find out where they are."

Chewbacca growled and reached with his long hairy arm to toggle a few switches on the *Millennium Falcon*'s control panel.

Han fired two warning shots. Bolts of brilliant light streaked past the squarish planar wings of the Imperial craft—bracketing it, but doing no damage.

"Attention, TIE pilot," Han said. "You're going nowhere if I don't find out where . . ." He paused. ". . . the two young Jedi Knights are. You're in the middle of my targeting cross, so your choices are simple: surrender, or we blow you out of the sky."

A gruff voice came back over the comm systems. "Surrender is betrayal," the pilot said, then broke the connection.

The TIE fighter zoomed upward on an impossibly steep trajectory, climbing into the air above the dense green treetops. Then the Imperial ship wheeled about in an evasive maneuver.

"All right," Han said, his anger evident. "This old ship has taken on plenty of TIE fighters in its day. We can take on one more. Punch it, Chewie."

The *Falcon* lunged forward in another burst of speed as Chewbacca worked the controls.

Em Teedee wailed, "Oh, no! I can't watch. Somebody cover my optical sensors."

Han spared a second to glance back at the droid, and found Lowbacca cradling Em Teedee in his lap. "Just like having See-Threepio with us again. I think we may have to adjust that programming."

"Oh, dear," Em Teedee said.

In the back Lowbacca grumbled a suggestion, which his uncle seconded loudly.

"Good idea," Han said. "Let's try the tractor beam first. Maybe—just maybe—we can bring that ship to the ground without destroying it. That way we can get some information. If we say 'Please,' he might be a little more cooperative."

Chewbacca worked the *Falcon*'s tractor beam generator, casting out the invisible beam like a force-field net to grab the Imperial ship.

The TIE fighter lurched and jerked to one side as the tractor beam snagged a partial hold—but the pilot alternated bursts from his twin ion engines and tore free, spinning upward in a tight corkscrew that made Han whistle with reluctant admiration.

"This guy's good," he said. "After him, Chewie! Full speed."

The TIE fighter, as if seeing it as his one chance for escape, darted back down toward the rough greenery of Massassi trees. It dodged jagged branches that thrust up like blackened witches' fingers where lightning and forest fires had burned the jungle, dipped down to trace the winding courses of rivers, and streaked over lush canyons—all with the *Millennium Falcon* following in hot pursuit.

If it were only a matter of speed, the *Falcon*'s more powerful engines could have outrun the TIE fighter and brought it down, but the small ship's maneuverability among the dangerous treetops gave the Imperial pilot a definite advantage.

Han Solo, however, had greater determination. "What have you done with my kids?" he yelled into the comm channel.

It was obvious he expected no answer, but to everyone's surprise, the pilot spoke back in a calculating voice. "They are your children, pilot? They were alive when I left them—but the jungle is a dangerous place. There's no telling if they will last long enough for you to rescue them."

Tenel Ka marveled at the brilliant strategy. "It's a trick," she said. "He wants you to break off the pursuit."

"I know," Han said, glancing back at her. His face was ashen. "But what if it's true?"

The TIE pilot used Han's brief hesitation to take his last best chance for escape: arrowing upward and bolting straight toward space. The twin ion engines roared through the thinning atmosphere.

Chewbacca yelped in reaction. Without waiting for Han to give the order, the Wookiee copilot pushed the accelerators to maximum. The *Falcon*, white heat rippling from its rear sublight engines, zoomed after the TIE fighter.

The acceleration slammed Tenel Ka back against her seat, and she grimaced as the tug of additional gravities stretched her skin. She squeezed her eyes shut. Beside her, Lowbacca grunted with the strain, but Han and Chewie seemed accustomed to putting such stress on their bodies.

The bright, milky-blue sky grew darker, turning a deep purplish color around them as they soared upward. The stars shone out as the *Falcon* pulled into the night of space. The blurry sphere of the great orange gas giant Yavin filled most of their cockpit windows.

The TIE fighter zigzagged to throw off pursuit, shifting course at random intervals and burning a great deal of energy.

"Maybe we can still wound his ship and pull him in," Han said, his voice strained.

Chewbacca piloted the *Falcon* as Han controlled the weapons systems. "I can't get a target lock," Han said.

The TIE fighter zoomed above the green jewel of the jungle moon.

Arching around in a tight orbit, the *Falcon* clung to it, following closely. Han fired repeatedly with his laser cannons—but the scarlet bolts missed.

Han pounded his fist on the control panel. "Hold still for a minute!" he shouted.

Then, as if obliging, the TIE fighter paused in the middle of the weapons system's aim-point grid. The target lock flashed brightly, and Han gave a whoop of excitement.

"Gotcha!" he said, and depressed both sets of firing studs.

But at the last possible instant, the lone TIE fighter shot forward with a blaze of astonishing speed, becoming a molten metal point of light. It dwindled in the sudden distance, screaming forward with instant lightspeed—and plunged into hyperspace with a silent bang.

"It's not my fault," Han Solo said, gaping at the vanished target. He let his shaking hands fall away from the firing controls. "A TIE fighter doesn't have lightspeed engines! It's a short-range ship."

Lowbacca grumbled an explanation, and Tenel Ka nodded.

"Jaina did *what*?" Han said in disbelief. "But that hyperdrive was for her to tinker with, not to install. She's got a lot of explaining to do with I see her—" He broke off, suddenly realizing where the twins were.

"Forget the TIE fighter. Let's go get the twins!" he said.

He changed the *Falcon*'s course and arrowed straight back down to the emerald-green sphere of the jungle moon of Yavin.

# 22

BACK AT THE tiny jungle clearing where the wreck of the TIE fighter had rested for two decades, Jacen and Jaina decided that their best chance for rescue lay in climbing to the treetops—no matter how difficult it might be. From that height, they could spot any incoming ships and set up some sort of signal.

Before leaving, they scrounged at the crash site and at Qorl's old encampment for whatever they could possibly find useful, then stuffed it in their packs. Their Jedi training had taught them to be resourceful.

Remembering how they had used the Force to help them scale the Great Temple with Tenel Ka, the twins found a Massassi tree with plenty of densely interwoven branches and hanging vines. They stared upward, then at each other, before beginning the long, sweaty climb. Jacen and Jaina were scratched up and aching and smeared with forest debris by the time they made it to the top—but to their surprise, they felt invigorated by their accomplishment.

Up in the canopy in a thick nest of tangled branches, they tried to light a leafy fire to send a beacon of smoke into the sky. Jacen collected leaves and twigs and piled them onto a curved piece of plasteel left over from their repairs on the TIE fighter.

Jaina had brought Tenel Ka's flash heater, but the charge was low. When the finger-sized unit sputtered and flashed, sending out a few last sparks, she took the back panel off and used her multitool to tinker with the circuits. By pumping up the power output, she produced one last flash that set the pile of fresh branches on fire.

The lush green leaves burned slowly, and the fire would not gain enough heat to become a bright blaze. But, as they had hoped, a satisfying gray-blue smoke curled upward, a clear signal for anyone who was looking.

Even so, they couldn't be certain that anyone would know where to look. Unless Lowbacca or Tenel Ka had managed to get back to the academy, no one would have any idea where to begin a search.

"Guess it might be a good idea next time if we let someone know where we're going and what we're doing, huh?" Jaina said, staring up at the discouragingly empty blueness.

"Probably," Jacen agreed, settling himself beside her on the branches. Sweat ran down his face as he rested his chin on his grimy hands. "Want to hear another joke?"

"No," Jaina answered firmly. She wiped her damp forehead with the sleeve of her now-ragged jumpsuit, and continued scanning the skies. She shifted beside him, feeling the breeze and listening to the whisper of millions of leaves.

Jacen fed more leaves to the fire.

Suddenly, Jaina sat up straight. "Look!" she said, pointing up. A white starpoint grew brighter, glittering silver. Ripples of sound from a sonic boom echoed like thunder across the sky of Yavin 4. "It's a ship."

Jacen closed his liquid-brown eyes and smiled. Then the twins blinked and looked at each other. "The *Falcon*," they said in unison.

"Can Dad sense us?" Jacen asked.

"I don't think so," Jaina said. "At least not with the Force. But wait . . ." She closed her eyes again, reaching out with what she knew of Jedi powers. "Lowie's with him!"

"And Tenel Ka, too," Jacen said. "They're all right!"

Jaina laughed with relief. "Did you expect any less from a young Jedi Knight?"

The *Falcon* must have spotted their smoke, and now headed toward them. High in the branches, the twins stood and waved. As it approached, the blaster-scarred light freighter seemed the most beautiful machine they had ever seen.

The big ship hovered over them with a gust of its repulsorlifts. Branches blew away beneath them, but Jacen and Jaina held their positions, reaching upward as the bottom access hatch of the *Falcon* popped open.

Chewbacca's hairy arm dangled down, grabbing Jacen's hands and pulling him up into the ship as if he were a piece of lightweight luggage. A moment later, Lowie's ginger-furred arms reached out to help Jaina up.

Han scrambled from the cockpit, rushing to scoop up both of his children in a big hug. "You're alive—you're not hurt!" he said, looking them over with anxious relief. "Sorry I'm late."

"It's all right," Jacen answered. "We knew you'd come."

Tenel Ka and Lowie also greeted the twins, with hugs all around and enthusiastic thumps on the back.

"Oh, hooray!" Em Teedee's tinny voice chimed in. "This *is* cause for a celebration."

"Let's get back to the Jedi academy first; I'm sure everyone's been worried about us," Han said. "I think we need to tell about a few adventures."

• • •

A few days later, after the *Falcon* carried the T-23 back from where it had crashed in the treetops, Lowbacca and Jaina worked in the shadow-draped courtyard of the Great Temple, tinkering with the damaged skyhopper. Jaina poked her grease-smeared face up out of the engine compartment and looked around.

She watched as Jacen scurried across the landing field out front, low to the ground, trying to catch an eight-legged lizard crab he wanted to add to his collection. Leaves and broken blades of grass were tangled in his tousled hair, as usual. The creature darted left and right, trying to find a hiding place among the close-cropped weeds of the landing field.

Spying a large shady spot, the lizard crab scuttled for shelter out of reach under the T-23. Jaina giggled as Jacen pulled up short just in time to keep from banging his head against the skyhopper's hull.

With a shrug, he leaned against the craft and brushed the dirt from his jumpsuit. "Oh well," he said, grinning. "Next time."

"As long as you're just standing there, could you please hand me a hydrospanner?" Jaina said.

Jacen bent and rummaged in the tool kit on the grass, then handed the tool up.

"You concentrate on the onboard computer systems, Lowie," Jaina said, discussing repair strategies. "That's what you're best at." At the Wookiee's growl of agreement, she added, "Don't worry about these engines. I'll have them running again in no time."

"Mind if I join you?" a calm voice said from behind her.

"Uncle Luke!" Jaina cried, jumping up and turning toward him. "When did you get back?"

"Only this morning," Luke Skywalker said, looking admiringly at the vehicle. "Could you use any help? I'm pretty good with these little air speeders, you know." He smiled as if savoring a fond memory. "I had a ship a little like this once . . . my own T-16 skyhopper when I was growing up on—"

Just then, Tenel Ka emerged from the large lower door of the Great Temple. The cool underlevels had once stored the Rebel base's X-wing fighters.

"Excuse me for a moment," Luke said, and turned to raise his hand in a warm greeting. He strode over to Tenel Ka and spoke to her for a long while as if she were an old friend. Being with the great Jedi Master caused the young girl from Dathomir to look uncharacteristically intimidated.

"Well, what are we waiting for?" Jaina asked the others. She opened an inner access panel with her multitool and began running diagnostics on the T-23's engines. Jacen surreptitiously scanned the cropped grass and weeds, looking for another specimen to catch.

Lowbacca snared a tangle of wires from the cockpit control panels and began sorting them by color and function. He murmured to himself as he worked, and Jacen could hear Em Teedee start to speak. At a *clunk* of something metal hitting the floor plates, Jacen stuck his head into the T-23. Lowbacca had accidentally dropped Em Teedee from his belt again.

The miniature translating droid began scolding the young Wookiee at high volume. "Really, Master Lowbacca, do try to be careful! You've dropped me again, and that's simply careless. How would you like it if *your* head detached and kept falling on the ground? I am an extremely valuable piece of equipment and you ought to take better care of me. If my circuits become damaged I won't be able to translate, and then where will you be? I can't believe—"

With a grunt, Lowbacca switched off Em Teedee, and then made a satisfied sound.

Jacen looked up to see Jaina staring at the deep blue sky. He followed her gaze and knew exactly what she was thinking. "Do you suppose Qorl ever made it back home?"

"If he does, I wonder if he'll find what he expects when he gets there," she answered. "He would have been better off staying with us."

When they noticed Luke Skywalker and Tenel Ka strolling back toward the T-23, Lowie and Jaina climbed out of the dismantled cockpit to stand next to Jacen.

Luke looked at the battered air speeder and ran his fingertips over its smooth hull. "Back on Tatooine I used to roar through Beggar's Canyon in my own T-16, chasing down womp rats."

Jacen and Jaina looked at their uncle, amazed and unable to imagine the introspective Jedi Master as a hotshot daredevil pilot.

Luke's lips curved in a wistful smile. "That was a whole different life from now." He turned to the young Jedi Knights. "When you get this thing fixed, I'd like to go for a ride with you. If that's all right."

They looked at him in astonishment. Lowie muttered something indecipherable and cleared his throat nervously.

"I hope you're fitting in here, Lowbacca," Luke said, nodding toward the young Wookiee. "I know it's difficult to go away from home and stay in a strange place, but I see you've made some new friends."

He looked at the others. "I'm proud of you all," Luke said. "You did a fine job under very trying circumstances, even when I wasn't here to guide you. You have a lot of potential—but becoming a Jedi Knight takes a great deal of hard work and practice."

The students nodded. "This is a fact," Tenel Ka said solemnly.

"You're young, and there are many things you could do with your lives," Luke said. "Are you certain you still want to become Jedi Knights?"

Their enthusiastic shouts rang out in unison. Lowbacca's loud bellow was so emphatic that even with Em Teedee switched off, none of the others needed a translation.

**The dark side of the Force
has a new training ground . . .**

**STAR WARS
YOUNG JEDI KNIGHTS**

# Shadow Academy

The Dark Jedi Brakiss—the student Luke Skywalker expelled from his academy—has learned much since he left. Enough to master the dark side of the Force. And enough to establish his own school for training Jedi—the Shadow Academy.

But now Brakiss has been given an even greater task. Not only must he create a sinister legion of Dark Jedi to serve the Empire, he must undertake a challenge not even Darth Vader and the Emperor could meet: Kidnap the heirs of the Skywalker bloodline, and turn them to the dark side of the Force . . .

Turn the page for a special preview of the next book in the STAR WARS: YOUNG JEDI KNIGHTS series:
**Shadow Academy**
Available now!

LANDO CALRISSIAN RUSHED toward the control bridge of GemDiver Station. "Come on, kids. Follow me!" he shouted.

Jaina took the lead, while Lowie and Jacen followed at a run. Lowie's long Wookiee legs made him practically plow over Lando in his haste. "Oh, *do* be careful, Lowbacca!" Em Teedee called.

Taking a turbolift to the upper observation tower, they bustled onto the control bridge, a cylindrical turret that protruded above the main armored body of GemDiver Station. Narrow rectangular windows encircled the control room, allowing a full view in all directions. Directly below each windowport sat glowing diagnostic screens, many of which flashed alarm warnings. Lando's armed guards ran about, strapping additional weapons to their belts, preparing for an external assault.

"We are under attack, sir," Lobot murmured in his quiet, difficult-to-hear voice.

The cyborg was a blur of motion, his hands darting from keyboard to keyboard, scanning the screens around him and silently assessing details. The lights on the computer implants at the sides of his head flashed like fireworks.

Lando scanned the narrow observation windows and saw the fleet of ships coming in from deep space. "Do you think they're pirates?" he asked. Then he said reassuringly to the twins and Lowie, "Don't worry. We've got station security on alert. They don't have a chance against our defenses."

Jaina studied one of the diagnostic screens, and pursed her lips. She shook her head. "Not just pirates," she said, recognizing the ellipsoid shape of the main body, engine turrets swept back like jagged wings on top and bottom. "Imperial craft. The four on the outside are Skipray blastboats, each fully equipped with three ion cannons, proton torpedo launcher, concussion missiles, and two fire-linked laser cannons." She looked calmly up at Lando's surprised expression. "Dad had me study a lot of ships. Believe me, these're more than even your security systems could hope to fight."

Lando clapped a hand to his forehead and groaned. "That's not just a pirate fleet, that's an armada! What's the big ship in the middle? I don't recognize it."

In her mind Jaina ran through mechanical specifications of all the ship designs she had learned from her father. Han Solo had enjoyed spending time helping his daughter study how starships worked—but right now she was at a loss.

"Some kind of modified assault shuttle, maybe?" Jaina said. Through the magnification on the screens they stared as the ships came relentlessly in. "But I don't understand that contraption in the bow."

The mysterious assault shuttle had a strange device mounted at its front end, circular and jagged, like the wide-open mouth of a fanged underwater predator.

"Send a distress signal," Lando said to Lobot. "Full spectrum. Make sure *everybody* knows we're under attack here."

With maddening computer-enhanced calm, Lobot shook his bald head. "I already tried. We're jammed, sir—can't punch a signal through their screens."

"Well, what do they want?" Lando said in exasperation.

"They've made no demands," Lobot replied. "They refuse to answer our hails. We do not know what they're after."

Jaina stared out the window at the incoming ships and felt cold inside. She shuddered. Next to her Jacen squeezed her hand, frowning in anxiety. They had both realized the same thing.

"I've got a bad feeling about this," Jacen said. "It's us they want, isn't it?"

"Yeah, I can feel it," Jaina said, her voice barely above a whisper. Lowie nodded his shaggy head and groaned in agreement.

"What do you kids mean?" Lando looked at them with surprise in his large brown eyes. "They *must* be after our corusca gems—it's the only thing that makes sense."

Jaina shook her head confidently, but Lando was too busy to pay further attention. The four flanking blastboats spread out from the central assault shuttle toward the defensive satellites surrounding GemDiver Station.

"Have you removed the fail-safes from the targeting systems?" Lando asked.

Lobot nodded. "Systems ready to fire," he murmured. High-powered lasers from the defensive satellites lanced out toward the blastboats; but the small satellites could not generate enough power to penetrate the heavy Imperial armor.

Each Skipray blastboat targeted one of the small satellites and unleashed a crackling blur from its ion cannons. The defensive satellites powered up, preparing to fire again. But then, all the lights went dead.

"The ion cannons fried their circuits," Lobot announced in his calm voice. "They are all offline."

The Skiprays came in for another strike

and fired with laser cannons, this time blasting the defensive satellites into molten metal vapor.

"We've still got the station's armor," Lando said, but his trembling voice betrayed his lack of confidence.

The modified assault shuttle in the middle of the armada homed in on one of the lower space doors. From the bottom decks of the station came a loud *thump* and *clang* as something large and heavy struck the outer hull—and stayed.

"What are they doing?" Lando asked.

"The modified assault shuttle has attached itself to the outer wall of GemDiver Station," Lobot reported.

"Where?"

The bald cyborg checked readings. "One of the equipment bays. I think they're trying to force their way in."

Lando waved his hand in dismissal. "Well, they can knock but they can't come in." He smiled nervously. "Just keep all the airlocks sealed. Our armor should hold."

"Excuse me," Jaina said, "but I just figured out what that modification is. I think they plan to bore through the station walls. The jagged things we saw looked like teeth—so I'm guessing they cut through metal."

"Not *this* metal." Lando shook his head. "The station wall is double armored. Nothing could cut through it."

Jacen piped up. "I thought you said corusca gems could cut through anything."

Lando shook his head again. "Sure, but that would take a whole shipment of industrial-grade corusca gems." Then he stopped, eyes widening. "Well, uh, we *have* shipped some industrial-grade gems since we upgraded our operations."

He picked up an intercom wand and spoke into it. "This is Lando Calrissian. All security details go to lower equipment bay number—" He leaned over Lobot's shoulder to look at the screen. "—number thirty-four. Full armor and weapons. We're about to be boarded by hostile forces."

Lando took a blaster pistol from the sealed armory case inside the bridge deck. He turned to Lobot. "*Nobody* boards my station without my permission." He started down the corridor, calling over his shoulder as he ran. "You kids find a safe place and stay there!"

So of course the young Jedi Knights followed him.

Station guards in padded dark-blue uniforms sprinted from corridor intersections. The pastel colors and nature sounds of Gem-Diver Station seemed oddly out of place, no longer soothing amid the chaos of defensive preparations and the turmoil of screeching alarms.

By the time they reached lower equipment

bay 34, a squad of station guards had already set up their position behind storage containers and supply modules, blaster rifles drawn and aimed at the wall.

Jaina heard a whining, gnawing sound that made her teeth vibrate. A circular section of the outer wall glowed, and she could imagine the modified assault shuttle on the other side, linked to GemDiver Station like a huge battle-ready brine-eel, chewing its way through the station armor.

A bright white line appeared in the circle as a corusca tooth bit through the thick plate. Jaina wondered belatedly if the attacking ship's seal against the station was tight. What if the air in the equipment bay started to bleed off into the vacuum of space? But it was too late to worry about that now.

One of Lando's station guards, keyed up with overwhelming tension, let off two shots from his blaster rifle. The bolts spanged against the wall and left a discolored blotch on the inner hull, but the jaws of the boring machine continued to chew through the plates.

In a flash, with a puff of steam and the *crump* of small, shaped explosives, a large disk of the outer hull fell forward into the equipment bay.

Lando's security forces stared firing immediately, even before the smoke cleared, but the enemy on the other side did not pause. Dozens of white-armored Imperial stormtroopers boiled through the hole like a hive of frenzied myrmins that Jacen had once kept in his collection of exotic pets. The stormtroopers fired as they charged—using only the curving blue arcs of stun beams, Jaina was relieved to see.

Four stormtroopers went down with smoking holes in their white armor; but more and more kept coming from the assault shuttle. The air in the equipment bay was crisscrossed with bright weapons fire.

Looming behind the armed stormtroopers, cloaked in shadows and rising smoke, stood a tall and sinister woman dressed in a black cape with spines on each shoulder. She had flowing ebony hair like the wings of a bird of prey. Despite her growing terror, Jaina saw that the woman's eyes were a striking purple, like the violet of iridescent jungle flowers on Yavin 4. Jaina felt her heart clench as if hands of ice had wrapped around it.

The ominous dark woman stepped through the smoldering hole in the wall of GemDiver Station, oblivious to the weapons fire. A faint electric-blue corona of static lightning clung around her like the powerful discharges that had zapped the *Fast Hand* in the atmospheric storms of Yavin.

"Don't harm the children," the woman

shouted. Her voice was slow and heavy, but razor-sharp menace edged every word.

At the mention of the children, Lando whirled to see that the twins and Lowie had followed him. "What are you doing here?" he said. "Come on, we've got to get you to safety!" He waved his blaster pistol toward the entryway. Then, as if in afterthought, he turned and fired three more times, catching one of the stormtroopers full in the chest armor.

Jacen and Jaina bolted down the corridor. Lowie, needing no further encouragement, bellowed as he ran along.

Lando came charging after. "I guess you were right," he said, panting. "For some reason they *are* after you."

"I'm just a simple droid," Em Teedee wailed. "I hope they don't want me."

A series of muffled explosions erupted behind them, and a shockwave of heat rippled through the station's metal corridors, making them stumble.

Lando caught his balance and steadied Jaina. "Turn right, up here," he gasped.

They ran. More blaster fire followed them, then a third explosion. Lando clenched his teeth. "This has *not* been a good day," he grumbled.

"I most heartily concur," Em Teedee chimed from Lowie's waist.

"Here, in the shipping chamber." Lando gestured for the three to stop outside the barricaded door of the launching room where they had seen the cargo pods and the droids packing corusca gems for automated shipment.

Lando punched in an access code with trembling fingers. A red light blinked. "ACCESS DENIED." Lando hissed something, then re-keyed the number. This time the light winked green, and the heavy triple doors sighed open. Inside, the two copper-colored droids continued packing the hyperpods. "Excuse me," one droid said, sounding flustered, "could you please discontinue that racket? The noise makes it difficult for us to process."

Lando ignored the droids as he pushed the kids inside. "We can't get you away from here—those blastboats would come after you before you knew it—but this is the safest place on the station. I'll stand outside and guard the door." He gripped his blaster pistol, feigning confidence.

Lowie growled, obviously wanting to fight; but before Jacen or Jaina could say anything, Lando slapped the emergency panel. The thick doors clanged shut, locking them inside the chamber.

Jacen placed his ear against the thick door and listened, but he could hear only the muffled noises of battle. Lowie, his ginger-colored fur standing on end with battle readiness, kneaded his big knuckles. Jaina looked around the room for anything to help them fight.

Jacen yelled to the copper-colored droids, "Hey, is there an armory in here? Do you have any weapons?"

The droids paused and swiveled smooth copper heads toward him, optical sensors glowing. "Please do not disturb us, sir," they said, resuming their tasks. "We have work to do."

Outside the door, the sound of sudden gunfire increased. Jaina pulled Jacen back from the door as she heard Lando shout. The door vibrated with energy bolts, then suddenly everything went quiet. She waited, backing away and looking into her twin brother's brandy-brown eyes. They both swallowed. Lowbacca let out a thin sound like a whimper. The multi-armed droids continued working, undisturbed.

A shower of sparks ran around part of the door as heavy-duty lasers cut into it, slicing away a section.

"D'you suppose you could invent some sort of weapon for us in the next few seconds?" Jacen said.

Jaina racked her brain for inspiration, but her inventiveness failed her.

The door split open, melted and smoking.

The security breach set off yet another alarm, but the sounds were pitiful and superfluous in the already-overwhelming noise of the battle for GemDiver Station.

Stormtroopers muscled their way in.

The two packing droids trundled indignantly toward the stormtroopers. "Intruder alert," one of the droids said. "Warning. No unauthorized entry is permitted. You must return to—"

In response, the stormtroopers fired with all their weapons, blasting both copper droids into shards of smoking components that clattered and sparked on the floor.

Jaina saw Lando sprawled unconscious on the floor outside the door, his green cape pooled around him. His right arm extended forward, still grasping the blaster pistol.

The towering dark woman strode in, her violet eyes flashing at the three companions. The stormtroopers leveled blaster pistols at Jacen, Jaina, and Lowbacca.

"Wait!" Jaina said. "What do you want?"

"Do not let them manipulate your minds," the dark woman cried to the stormtroopers. "Stun them!"

Before Jaina could say anything else, bright blue arcs shot toward them.

Jaina fell into blackness.